E VALLEY OF THE SHADOW

Books by George G. Gilman in the STEELE series available from New English Library:

ADAM STEELE 1: THE VIOLENT PEACE
ADAM STEELE 2: BOUNTY HUNTER
ADAM STEELE 3: HELL'S JUNCTION
ADAM STEELE 4: VALLEY OF BLOOD
ADAM STEELE 5: GUN RUN
ADAM STEELE 6: THE KILLING ART
ADAM STEELE 7: CROSS-FIRE
ADAM STEELE 8: COMMANCHE CARNAGE
ADAM STEELE 9: BADGE IN THE DUST
ADAM STEELE 10: THE LOSERS
ADAM STEELE 11: LYNCH TOWN
ADAM STEELE 12: DEATH TRAIL
ADAM STEELE 13: BLOODY BORDER
ADAM STEELE 14: DELTA DUEL
ADAM STEELE 15: RIVER OF DEATH
ADAM STEELE 16: NIGHTMARE AT NOON
ADAM STEELE 17: SATAN'S DAUGHTERS
ADAM STEELE 18: THE HARD WAY
ADAM STEELE 19: THE TARNISHED STAR
ADAM STEELE 20: WANTED FOR MURDER
ADAM STEELE 21: WAGONS EAST
ADAM STEELE 22: THE BIG GAME
ADAM STEELE 23: FORT DESPAIR
ADAM STEELE 24: MANHUNT
ADAM STEELE 25: STEELE'S WAR: THE WOMAN
ADAM STEELE 26: STEELE'S WAR: THE PREACHER
ADAM STEELE 27: STEELE'S WAR: THE STOREKEEPER
ADAM STEELE 28: STEELE'S WAR: THE STRANGER
ADAM STEELE 29: THE BIG PRIZE
ADAM STEELE 30: THE KILLER MOUNTAINS
ADAM STEELE 31: THE CHEATERS
ADAM STEELE 32: THE WRONG MAN
ADAM STEELE 33: THE VALLEY OF THE SHADOW

EDGE MEETS ADAM STEELE: TWO OF A KIND
EDGE MEETS ADAM STEELE: MATCHING PAIR

The Valley of the Shadow

George G. Gilman

NEW ENGLISH LIBRARY

for:
Ken Bulmer –
a secret whisky drinker!

A New English Library Original Publication, 1983

First NEL Paperback Edition March 1983

NEL Books are published by
New English Library,
Mill Road, Dunton Green,
Editorial office: 47 Bedford Square, London WCIB 3DP

Typeset by PRG Graphics Redhill
Printed in Great Britain by
Cox & Wyman, Reading

0 450 05557 4

One

THE MAN who lay, sprawled on his back, in a sandy hollow at the foot of a timbered slope beside a little used trail in northern California, kept coming to and going from a state not far removed from consciousness. But during the late morning and into the mid-afternoon of this pleasantly warm fall day he did not make any further progress toward awareness of his surroundings. But neither did he show that he got any closer to death from the gangrene infected bullet wound in his upper right chest.

The only movement he made – beyond the shallow but regular rise and fall of his chest to breathe – was to alter the set of his features each time he seemed on the verge of coming awake. To display a grimace that gradually faded from his face as the intensity of what caused his pain subsided and he sank fully back into merciful oblivion.

It was the face of a man about forty. Clearly handsome despite the growth of bristles over several days, the ingrained dirt that had accumulated during the same period and the unflattering expressions that changed so often from grimaces to impassiveness and back again. The bristles were a mixture of red and white, indicating that the overly long and dishevelled hair of the man had once been auburn – before every strand became prematurely bleached. The skin beneath the bristles and ingrained with the dirt was stained dark by exposure to the elements and was deeply lined with more crinkles than could be blamed on the passing of the years. It was stretched taut over the man's regularly honed features based on a bone structure that was very sparsely fleshed.

His frame, which was clothed in a city style suit and sheepskin topcoat much the worse for wear, was likewise lean. And he was not tall. No more than a half inch above five feet six inches when standing at his full height, minus his spurless riding boots.

But it was a long time since this man had stood erect and, had he regained full consciousness while he was sprawled in the spread eagled attitude in the sandy hollow, he would not have given much for his chances of ever again standing upright. For this man was Adam Steele who was nothing if not a realist: and he would only have had to be briefly aware of the ugly stench of gangrene under his nostrils and to recall the circumstances which brought him to this place to know that the odds against him surviving were maybe longer than they had ever been during a life in which the threat of death was seldom absent from him.

Sometimes, though, the situation was not so black as it appeared – especially if a man was incapable of rational thought for more than a few seconds at a time. Which was how it had been at Golden Hill, a grim mining community just five miles east of where he now lay close to death, a day and a half ago. The poison erupted by the untreated bullet wound had already been distributed throughout his body in his bloodstream by the time he rode deliriously into the place where every citizen bar one mistook him for somebody else. And, instead of getting to see a doctor who would fix up the bullet wound for him, the Virginian found himself with a lynch rope encircling his neck: as he sat astride his chestnut mare under Golden Hill's hanging tree.

Now, in the sandy hollow between the wooded hill to the east and the narrow trail to the west, he was intermittently visited by isolated recollections of the recent past that his mind rejected almost immediately they entered it: as if in a series of attempts to prevent the badly injured man from being disturbed. But these attempts failed and Adam Steele was often brought to within a hairsbreadth of having to face up to harsh reality. Before physical agony which had its source in the wound, or the mental anguish of knowing – even while unconscious – the full extent of his desperate situation, came to reinforce the involuntary efforts of his mind and he was sucked back into the warm darkness of total insensibility. Until the next time, when the grimace revealed that the struggle had been resumed. A struggle between the two sides of Adam Steele, one which the man himself – with his wits about him – would have probably denied had any kind of existence any more.

Which did not conflict with him being a realist for, when he had his wits about him, the Adam Steele who was sprawled out under the California sun could – with justification for most of the time – consider that the Adam Steele of long ago in Virginia was extinct.

The War between the States had sown the seeds of the destruction of the Virginian gentleman and the violent peace of war's aftermath had nurtured the kind of man who replaced the first one.

Benjamin P. Steele had been among the wealthiest of the Virginian plantation owners before the war. And one of the most respected of his kind. A widower with an only son upon whom he showered the best of everything. But Adam Steele was not the kind of boy, youth and young man to allow himself to be spoiled, and he regulated his indulgences in the better things of life. Was not a dandy by Eastern standards and did not misuse the privileges of wealth. Strove to be worthy of taking his father's place in both the professional and the social spheres and to gain as much respect among business associates and friends as his father commanded.

But in the war Ben Steele gave covert support to the Union while Adam rode as a cavalry lieutenant for the Confederacy. Both of them harbouring the hope – as did many other families divided by the same conflict of loyalties – that with the coming of peace the past could be forgotten and old resentments forgiven. And few were more eager than the Steele father and son for their own reconciliation after the Appomattox peace signing: anxious to be reunited and to return to the plantation where they would pick up the threads of their former way of life – and become the men they once had been.

It was not to be, however.

The father of the son who had escaped being lynched in a Californian mining town was not so fortunate back in Washington all those years ago. For, as part of the plot that led to the assassination of President Abraham Lincoln, Ben Steele was strung up from a beam in a bar room. Right across the street from Ford's Theatre where Booth shot Lincoln. The old man an innocent victim of the conspiracy as he took a drink while he awaited the arrival of his son.

Adam Steele looked not so different since before the war. And maybe he could have become what he once had been, had it not been necessary for him to cut down the corpse of his father from that bar room beam. And fire the opening shot of his personal violent peace. Before he took the body back to the burned out ruin that had once been home. There to bury it in the seared earth before he set out to track down and kill every man who had a hand in the lynching of his father. The instrument of ultimate vengeance a Colt Hartford revolving rifle with an inscribed plate on the right side of the stock – the inscription proclaiming that Abraham Lincoln had presented the weapon to Benjamin Steele as a mark of the President's appreciation for help given. This rifle the sole inheritance of son from a once immensely wealthy father, and even its rosewood stock was scorched from the fire that had rased the former great plantation.

The younger Steele had learned much about the primitive art of killing and the sometimes even cruder art of surviving while he rode the battlegrounds of the eastern states during the first half of the eighteen sixties. And on the manhunt that took him westward he was not emotionally prepared to accept that it was necessary to make compromises in such things now – to re-adapt, as he had been anxiously willing to do on his way to meet his father in Washington – to an older, wiser and maybe better version of the Adam Steele he had been when game was all he shot at.

The law should have taken care of the killers of Ben Steele. And when Adam Steele took the law into his own hands, the law in the form of Deputy Jim Bishop came to get him. Bish came a long way to find and arrest Steele. Two men who went back a long way – had been best friends in childhood and through adolescence. The friendship interrupted by war. Then ended in the violent peace in the worst way of all – when the one killed the other.

It was on that day in Tennessee that the Adam Steele of old became extinct and the new one – today so close to death in California – was conceived: and a few weeks later was born at the conclusion of a massive drinking jag at the cantina in a Mexican village called Nuevo Rio. From that squalid little community south of the border to the town of gold grubbers and whores called Golden Hill was some twelve hundred miles as the crow flies. But the new style Adam Steele had ridden a lot further than that in something over ten years to get from one place to the other. For no other reason than it was where each stretch of trail he rode led to in what was ultimately an aimless trek to keep from getting killed – by the law, his enemies, the elements or starvation.

For a while, at the outset, there had been other more materialistic goals at which he aimed. For the long days of drinking not only failed to blot out the remorse he felt for strangling Jim Bishop to death – they also did not wipe his memory clean of what life had been like for the old style Adam Steele. And so he sought to make enough money to start over anew an enterprise that might one day get to be as big as the Virginian plantation had been. Then he lowered his sights and searched for any place reminiscent of the lush Virginia countryside where he might be able to put down roots without ambition to expand beyond his original claim or title. But he was thwarted in the lesser aspiration, too. And, accepting that his destiny was to be that of a rootless drifter, he narrowed his wants to the few simple luxuries that could be available to a man leading such a wandering life. A good horse and equipment, fine clothing and – at stops along the way – the best food, accommodation and women he could afford.

But even these desires were doomed to be achieved only at the risk of being snatched away from him by his cruel ruling fate that seemed intent upon punishing him more severely than the man-made justice he had always escaped. And so he learned as he drifted to wish for nothing and to expect to have to fight to get and keep what he wanted. Took all else as it came and never wasted time and effort with regret for what was lost – temporarily or gone for ever. Was a dude by Western standards maybe – albeit invariably the worse for wear – who for most of the time did not misuse his privileged position as the complete outsider.

Now, in the afternoon sunlight, an expression that was not a grimace of physical pain or mental anguish appeared on the bristled, filthy face of the man coming close to consciousness. Incredibly, it was a smile that parted the lips fractionally and turned them up at each side: as Adam Steele's active mind in a punished body decided that it was better by far for a man to be detached from the kind of society that existed along the trails he rode than to be a member of it.

He came the closest yet to recovering consciousness and vented a muted cry of pain as he twitched the shoulder above the evil smelling wound. Which set two hungry flies making a meal of stale blood winging away as the smile became the more familiar grimace before the lean, element stained, experience and age lined face gradually resumed its look of impassiveness.

For several minutes his mind remained dormant while the essential physical functions that kept him alive continued their involuntary routine. But then his subconscious started to review the past again, and to concentrate on events of more recent origin. And the part he had played in these events which surely was directed by what had happened to him much further back in time?

He groaned and shook his head. Without grimacing and so feeling no pain now, as he made a gesture and sound of denial, expressing his unwillingness to get into an argument with himself about causes and effects. He was just one man, both as complex in some respect and as unsophisticated in others as the rest of his species. And he did what he did because at the time it appeared to him to be what was right – for himself. And if he made a mistake, he had to be ready to pay the price of the error without complaint.

It had seemed right not to kill the father and son of a man named Moses Jackson in the timber country of northern California. It was sufficient, he thought at the time, to simply divert the attention of the old man and the boy while he made a run for it. But the grandfather got off a shot to drive the .45 calibre bullet deep in the flesh of Steele's upper right chest.

For a while, his pride was hurt so much he overlooked the physical pain. He had been close to serious injury a thousand times in the war and after it. And always he avoided being hurt. Each narrow escape bolstering his confidence in a belief that his suffering was only ever to be of the emotional kind. That he would never be drastically incapacitated by a physical injury. And when at last he did stop the bullet it took him some time to come to terms with the fact. He had beaten his ruling fate on the emotional level and now he felt cheated that he was being attacked from an entirely different and so totally unexpected angle. Which was unfair.

But while he wrestled with the urge to whining self pity, a rational line of thought directed the course he follow. Not back the way he had come, to Six Rivers County. Where a bunch of homesteaders lived and where there was likely to be a medical practitioner of some kind. For Moses Jackson had been a homesteader in Six Rivers County and the Virginian was wanted for murdering him: and could be identified as the killer by the dead man's father and son. So, instead, Adam Steele rode through the rain in the opposite direction. Towards what had been his first objective of Golden Hill. Which also maybe had somebody who could tend the bullet wound. And where, for sure, there was some unfinished business to neaten up concerning a half breed Apache named Joseph Mitchell.

It was raining when he took the bullet in the chest. And it had stopped when he rode into Golden Hill. He had no way to gauge the passing of the time between the two events. Knew only that it was long enough for the open wound with the bullet in it to become gangrenous and for the poison to start a burning fever which allowed him only infrequent short periods of mental clarity. Sometimes he tumbled out of his saddle and at once hauled himself back up astride the mare again. At other times he lay where he fell. Slept or slipped into a fever triggered stupor. Always his horse was nearby. She was a fine mount. That was something he always tried to have even when he had abandoned hopes and desires for almost everything else – a good, strong animal to ride. Which was not a mere whim for a man like Adam Steele. But a necessity, to the same extent as food and water and a gun he could rely on.

A day, two days, three . . . ? At least two for the poison to have such an effect and the wound to smell so bad . . .

The grubbers for gold and the whores who took it away from them with much less effort mistook the almost unconscious Adam Steele for somebody else – one of their own kind. Who was wanted for murder, in the same way that the Virginian was really wanted in Six Rivers County. But down there they had law and order and a county seat called Fort Trinity where justice was dispensed by due process. At Golden Hill there was just the lynch rope tied to the hanging tree out at the end of the street beyond the bakery. Where the man the townspeople were convinced was Ethan Winston was taken to be hanged. And the half breed Apache named Joseph Mitchell – the only Golden Hill citizen who knew this was not Winston – had the task of lashing the rope to the stoutest branch of the oak.

But this blackest of situations had turned out not to be as it seemed at all – when the half breed Apache finished his business with Steele his own way.

Mitchell felt he owed the Virginian and now he repaid his debt: when the flat palm of the hand of an angrily impatient man came down with a sharp crack on the rump of the chestnut mare. The horse was normally level headed and docile, quick to respond to the commands of her rider. But her rider was in no position to give her a command on this dull, grey clouded morning. And the horse was unusually susceptible to panic: after at least two and a half days of submitting to the fever crazed wilfulness of Steele on the relentless trek through the deserted timber country, followed by the slow walk along the town street among the embittered crowd gathering to witness the hanging. A less intelligent animal would have been untouched by the contrast in conditions and remained unaffected by the grave awesomeness of the impending execution.

The slap acted to explode the tension that had been building in her equine brain. And this was manifested in the power of her forward lunge into a headlong gallop. That should have jerked her rider clear of the saddle and left him swinging violently from the stoutest branch of the Golden Hill hanging tree – lynched like his father before him a long time ago and a continent away. But the rope was not tied securely to the bough – by design, just as the half breed had promised. And, not entirely certain for several moments in the wake of the hanging gone wrong that he could believe what he had been told and what seemed to be happening to him, Adam Steele lacked the ability to even try to calm and then control his mount. Was too stunned by the turnabout which saved his life to take any hand in preserving it further. And stayed astride the galloping horse only by the instinctive actions of gripping more tightly the saddlehorn and thrusting his booted feet more firmly into the stirrups: in expectation of what should have been a futile defence against being wrenched off the back of the panicked mare.

The crowd screamed and cursed, raged and bellowed. The head of the Virginian was jerked fractionally backward by the briefly taut rope as the running knot came free of the branch. But he was only vaguely aware of this as a brief process of rational thought penetrated the stricture of mental shock. The half breed Apache really had set him free, for why else were the gold grubbers and the whores of this God-forsaken town so damn mad?

Then, just as he was about to take a positive hand in his own salvation, agony displaced the start of exhilaration and flooded through his every fibre. Its attack on his body causing his mind to be filled to capacity with responses to pain that would have plunged most men into deep unconsciousness. And for a long, anguished and agonised time the Virginian might have wished that he was like other men – had it been possible for him to indulge in such a voluntary exercise as wishful thinking.

But it was not possible for him to knowingly control anything about his being and what was happening to it during the time it took for the frightened chestnut mare to carry him along the tortuous route that was to end some five miles to the west of Golden Hill. For he was once again in the grip of that force that had steered him to his objective when he was delirious. A force which seemed to be even more powerful in the present circumstances as it demanded he not surrender to the counter command of his punished mind that he submit to unconsciousness and allow his agonised body the relief this would bring.

Just once during this headlong ride through the high, rugged timber country did he carry out a deliberate action of which he was perhaps aware. This when he shifted his right hand from its grip over the left on the saddlehorn, raised it to his throat, hooked the fingers inside the noose, tipped his head forward, pulled the circle of rope over his head and tossed the instrument of intended execution away. Then returned his right hand to his left on the horn. Was he conscious, in the two or three seconds it took to complete this act, of the chafing discomfort the encircling noose had caused? Or could such a relatively mild irritation be felt through the searing agony that streaked to his every nerve ending? And constantly triggered his latent powers of self preservation to will the muscles of his pain wracked body into doing what was necessary for him to remain on the back of the galloping, scared horse.

The trailing rope from the noose might well have snagged on some thorny bush or got caught in a cleft of rock so that he was jerked clear of the saddle. And maybe had his neck broken at the same time. Which would have been poetic justice. But maybe a disappointing end to the affair from the point of view of the people of Golden Hill. Who had not given chase to the runaway horse with the escaping rider after they were through screaming and yelling in high rage. So were doubtless confident that a lingering and painful death was all that awaited Adam Steele out in the deserted timber country. Which, the way they felt about him, had to strike them better than to have him die quick and easy on the rope as they had planned at first.

The Virginian groaned again. Louder than before, and the mere sound was sufficient to frighten off the returned flies. And the only move he made in addition to the regular ones of respiration was a flicker of his eyelids. But he did not open his eyes. He was conscious, though. Enough to be aware of his condition. And he held on to the final thought about Golden Hill. Knowing it had not come unbidden into his mind as a fragment of the past recalled by a fevered brain in an unfeeling body. Those images that had come and gone and often had brought him close to awareness had been recollections of events actually experienced. But in reflecting upon the actions and motives of the miners and whores of Golden Hill after he was long gone from the town, he had to be back in control of his mental processes again.

With his eyes still closed against the world he was ready to consciously re-enter, he allowed the guess about the Golden Hill people to slip away. And tensed himself for an expected wave of searing agony to sweep over him. But the sole sensation he experienced was of warmth that was far removed from the burning heat of fever. And now he recognised it for what it actually was – the pleasant gentleness of the sunshine on his face.

It had been a grey morning when they tried to hang him. Maybe a chill one. He could not remember. The same day as this one? It did not matter. He opened his eyes. Saw the cloudless blue of the sky. Then heard the thud of slow moving hooves and a gasp of shock.

He squeezed his eyes tightly closed again and struggled to prevent himself sinking into a deep slough of bitter depression. He had gotten away from those misguided people who had mistaken him for somebody else. And his highly developed talent for self preservation had stood him in good stead, even when he was not aware of what was happening to him. No, that was wrong! He could claim no credit for the escape. Joseph Mitchell set him free, the chestnut mare did the running and the people of Golden Hill elected not to give chase – or to abandon it after they lost sight of the sign.

But none of that mattered. Somewhere and sometime out along the aimless way taken by the mare, the rider slid or was thrown from the saddle. Could have been killed, but was not. Simply slumped unconscious. Could have died but had not. Lay for several hours – or maybe several days – feeling nothing for most of the time and occasionally showing signs of recovering awareness. But always previously retreating back into oblivion as he received a clue to just how badly his ruling fate had treated him this time. Now, though, encouraged by the lack of pain and the rational thought that he actually had made good his escape, he elected to stay in what seemed to be not such a bad state of waking.

No, that was wrong, too! He regained consciousness because he had been out for as long as his punished body and mind demanded and they were ready for him to face up to whatever lousy trick was lined up for him next.

And what this entailed was discovery and recapture by a searcher from Golden Hill. One of the many who had been sent out in every direction to locate the tracks of the runaway horse which in such a state of panic might head any place and toss off the rider at any time. Everyone was involved in the search. Men and women. Young and old. No, dammit! Wrong again!

'You know something, Bart?'

'Lotsa things, Arlene.'

'I think he's dead.'

'He ain't so. I can see him breathing. Can't you see him breathing?'

'Shoot, that's right! I can see it now.'

'Why don't you say shit instead of shoot, Arlene? When it's really shit you mean?'

'Because I'm a lady and ladies ain't supposed to use cuss words, Bart.'

'Shit, it's okay when Ma and Pa ain't around to hear you.'

During the monotone start of the exchange, Adam Steele thought he might have slipped back into unconsciousness. That his petulant reaction to discovery and imminent recapture was juvenile and in reaction to this his fevered mind had carried him back in imagination to an interlude in the distant past of his childhood in which a small girl was involved. But this lasted just a few seconds before the reality of what was taking place once again re-asserted a hold – firmer this time – on the mind of the Virginian. Who opened his eyes, turned his head a little towards the right and said:

'It's not okay, son. A lady doesn't use cuss words under any circumstances.'

For stretched seconds, while his eyes became adjusted to the brightness of the day, he saw just three blurred silhouettes – of a horse and two young children against the sky on the rim of the hollow. The kids seemed to be dressed indentically, but Arlene had much longer hair. She was to the right of the horse from Steele's viewpoint and had a hold on the reins.

'It sure is hard not to sometimes, mister,' she said. 'Like now. I'm thinking of a whole lot of them words.'

'We can't help what goes on in our minds,' Steele said and, as when he first spoke, did not recognise the rasping voice as his own.

'She's thinking them about you, mister,' Bart said. 'On account of you being alive when she hoped you'd be dead.'

He saw them clearly now. About ten years old.

Brother and sister, probably. With the no longer frightened chestnut mare between them.

'That's not very ladylike, Arlene,' Steele rasped. And grimaced as his sense of smell began to function and he caught the stench of the gangrene.

'I ain't got no horse, mister. Bart has and – '

'I let her ride him,' Bart put in defensively.

'Ain't the same as a person having a horse of her very own. And I figured that if you was dead, Ma and Pa would let me keep your horse. Of course, I'm real glad you ain't dead in every other way, but if you are gonna die soon, mister, may I have the mare?'

'Bart and Arlene Beamish!' a woman yelled angrily. 'So this is where you got to. Just what do you think you are doing there?'

Through teeth still gritted in the grimace of revulsion at the stink of himself, the Virginian murmured: 'Indulging in a little horseplay is all, ma'am.'

Two

NOBODY BUT Steele himself heard his soft spoken words. Not the brother and sister nor the irritated woman who came along the trail toward where they stood – turned away from the hollow to watch her approach. While the Virginian straightened his head to peer straight up at the sky again. Ignorant of whether this new turn of events was good or bad for him, but no longer tempted to indulge in self pity or to blame some ethereal ruler of his destiny for what had happened to him and this latest repercussion.

'My goodness, is that a strange horse you have there? You know you really should not go so far from the wagons. Your mother and the doctor have been worried sick. Why it is a strange horse! And it's saddled! Where is the owner . . . Oh, my goodness! What on earth has happened here?'

'He's real sick, seems to me, Miss Julia,' Arlene said, her total composure even more apparent in contrast to the abruptly shrill agitation of the adult. 'I was just asking him that should he die, if I might have the horse.'

'How could you, Arlene!' the woman snapped, less shrill but more shocked. 'You and Bart run this very minute to bring the doctor here! The wagons are right around the far side of the rise where they were when you wandered off! Go, tell him to be quick! Tell him the man was injured some time ago! That there's mortification of the wound!'

'Mortifi-what?' the young boy demanded.

'It's all poisoned up, Bart,' Arlene explained in a superior tone. 'That's why he smells so awful.'

'Go, go!' the woman urged.

Steele had been watching the scene on the rim of the hollow ever since the new arrival came into view. And could see the woman, the children and the horse in sharp focus now – as Miss Julia started down the gentle, thirty feet long, sandy slope and the Beamish brother and sister turned reluctantly away, Arlene leading the horse by the reins.

Both children made faces at the back of the concerned woman, who was quite obviously having some difficulty in not pulling a face of her own as she came closer to Steele and the stink of the gangrene strengthened its assault on her nostrils.

Arlene was slightly younger than her brother, he saw. Maybe ten to his eleven. And his first impression that they were dressed alike had been right in terms of the dungarees that each wore. And the small scale Stetsons on their heads, both of these black. But the girl's dungarees were grey over a pink shirt and the boy's were blue while his shirt was white. Both had absolutely straight hair, fair turning to brown, dark eyes, good teeth and tanned, freckle sprinkled complexions. They were maybe four and a half feet tall: beanpole thin, but not in an emaciated way. Bart looked like he was at the start of an outbreak of acne.

Miss Julia was about thirty and was also very thin, the loose fitting grey dress of some hard wearing fabric she had on giving no more than a mere indication that she thrust just a little at the chest and flared a little more at the hips. Elsewhere, the dress was buttoned at the wrist cuffs and at the throat, and its hem reached to the ankles of her black boots. She had a delicately pretty face with a fragile looking bone structure, pale skin that was almost translucent, a mouth that looked like it might have a petulant set in repose and round blue eyes that were magnified to maybe twice their true size by the lenses of her gold framed spectacles. Her hair, that fell in sweeping waves to perhaps six inches below the level of her narrow shoulders was a softer shade of yellow than the metal frames. She was perhaps fractionally shorter than he was, but probably weighed less than half what he did. So a very feminine female – the kind who looked ready to keel over if a man breathed on them.

But after she had conquered the threat of looking and maybe being nauseous, she seemed suddenly highly capable of taking charge of this situation which had caused her such distress only moments before.

'How long ago did this happen to you?' she asked in a tone that was as controlled as her expression and actions as she sank elegantly to her knees beside him.

'Three or four days, ma'am. Maybe even five or six.'

'You lost track of time?' Her lens magnified eyes shifted their cool gaze from the area of congealed blood and moist pus crusting and staining his sheepskin topcoat to examine the haggard and neglected planes of his face. Then extended a slender, long fingered hand to test the temperature of his forehead. 'You were feverish and now it has broken. A bullet wound?'

'Yes, ma'am.'

'Is there . . . was there any bleeding from the back?'

'The bullet's still inside me, ma'am. A .45 calibre fired from a revolver over more than just a few feet. Didn't have the punch to go on through, worst luck.'

He was trying not to grimace now. But it was no longer the smell of rotten flesh that bothered him. For the pain had started to make itself felt again – like the cool gaze of her eyes that had swept over the wound had a tangible substance that probed and prodded deep into the damaged tissue. And he talked – rasping out the words through his teeth in the strange sounding voice – to try to keep his mind occupied. Suspecting the pain he thought he experienced existed only in his mind: that the woman's fleeting examination had served to create an anticipatory sensation of the excruciating agony that was to come when the doctor arrived.

'Miss French is my name.'

'Adam Steele.'

'It's helping – to talk?'

'Yes.'

'I thought so. I couldn't tell for sure, though. It's difficult to judge, because you are obviously parched and . . . not comfortable. So it's not your normal voice. But I think I detect an accent of some description, Mr Steele. Not foreign, I think.'

'I am from Virginia. A time since I've been there. Still sounds in my voice. Reckon because I never stayed long enough in any other place for a different way of talking to catch on with me.'

'I'm from Chicago originally. Came out to Oregon with my parents fifteen years ago. Us and a whole lot of other folks. On our way down to the south of California right now. Us and Dr and Mrs Beamish and their two children. Father always was one for pastures new all the time. Never did settle for long any place in Oregon. The Beamish family, they . . . Oh, my goodness, you're going to have to excuse me while I'm – '

She powered up off her knees, coming erect so fast she almost overbalanced. And she stumbled several times but never actually fell as she moved at a scrambling run across the sandy slope from the trail. To plunge from sight into the timber at the base of the rise. Just made it into the trees before the bile hit her throat and she was forced to vomit.

This while Steele endured agony that was definitely real – having wrenched at the wound as he jerked his head to the side to follow the progress of Julia French. Wanting to apologise to her for the distress he had caused her and to tell her he understood that she, too, needed to prattle on about inconsequentials in order to keep herself under control. But even as he opened his mouth to call after her, he knew she was in no condition to comprehend what he intended to say to her. And then the bolt of pain shot viciously through him and he felt it was somehow very important that he should not give voice to it. So clamped his lips securely together, squeezed his eyes tightly closed, clenched his fists and tautened every muscle in his body: and kept the breath trapped in his lungs as a bead of sweat was squeezed from each pore. To run across exposed flesh and to soak into his clothing elsewhere. The first beads were followed by others and then still more. Seeming to extrude from him moisture in the same quantity as whatever it was that gushed at measured intervals from the gaping mouth of the nauseated woman in the timber. The sound of whose sickness Steele gradually came to hear as the imaginary shrillness of the scream he had kept trapped inside him faded down one of the countless dark corridors at the back of his abstracted mind. And the pain ebbed at the same pace, leaving him drenched in perspiration and with a sensation that there was not a single drop of moisture left inside him.

The sigh he vented sounded to him like the death rattle he had heard in the throats of so many men and women down the years. And he decided as he heard the sound and likened it to something it was not, he would have been content to have his life end here. Rather than in the wake of a whole lot more pain and discomfort caused by the ministrations of a doctor who was unlikely to be the best there was.

The sigh that sounded like a rattle went on a long time, as the woman up in the timber became quiet. And Steele knew he was no longer sighing. He began to relax now, every muscle except those that kept his eyelids compressed: as he peered into the self-imposed darkness and sought to identify the noise.

'Over there, Pa!' Bart Beamish yelled excitedly, like he was eager to be ahead of his sister in pointing out the place where the injured stranger lay.

And Steele recognised the creaking timbers and rolling wheels, with the clop of hooves sounding as well now, of a wagon on the trail to his right. Just as Arlene Beamish announced:

'Look, there's Miss Julia up in the trees, father. Maybe he died and she took him there to – '

'Sometimes I despair of the way your mother and I are raising you children in your case, young lady,' the man driving the wagon cut in on his daughter, in much the same imperturbable way she had spoken to him.

And he surveyed the badly injured man below him on the sand with a look of cool appraisal that was a match for the way Arlene had always eyed Steele, as he hauled on the reins to bring to a halt the big covered Studebaker. At the same point on the rim of the hollow from which everybody had first seen him. But the doctor, forewarned of what to expect and experienced in the horrors of injury and disease wasted no time in standing and looking from a distance. Reached into the back of the wagon to bring out his bag of medical supplies, leapt down from the vehicle and headed for his new patient in a series of moves that were both deliberate and rapid: totally lacking in any suggestion of bustling haste. And the way in which he issued commands was in keeping with this attitude.

'Julia, do not come down from there empty handed girl. Bring as much wood as you can carry. Dry, mind. Then go back and get more. Have your parents and Harriet assist you when they reach here. It should be soon. Bart, bring the cooking pot. Arlene, you will be in charge of getting water from barrel to pot.'

Beamish did not look at any of the trio as he addressed them, either to stress that he required the demands to be met immediately or to check that his children and the woman started to do his bidding. And as he drew closer to Steele, his unabashed interest in the helpless man's condition could be seen to intensify. He was about fifty, a six feet tall, more than two hundred pounds in weight man built on square lines – both his physique and his features. His hair, curly and unruly, was the mouse brown colour to which that on the heads of his children was changing. And the flecked near blackness of his eyes was another physical characteristic Arlene and Bart had inherited from him. But his jutting jaw and brow, his thick lipped mouth, his uneven teeth, his prominent nose and his heavy jowls had not so far shown any sign of being repeated in the facial structure of the youngsters. And they would need to grow up and outward a great deal for a few years before they displayed any genetic inclination to carry on a family resemblance to his frame. For which their mother was probably grateful – and the children, too, if they had yet developed the capacity to experience vanity. For Dr Beamish was both ugly and awkward looking. Which obviously troubled him not at all: for he affected sidewhiskers and a small pointed beard that added to rather than detracted from his forbidding countenance and wore clothing that seemed two sizes too small for him and so failed to disguise the unbecoming angularity of a body that appeared to lack co-ordination.

The MD's bedside manner was also a little rough around the edges as he thudded his bag heavily to the ground and folded down on to his haunches beside Steele – vented a low and long whistle that sounded suspiciously like admiration for the extent of the challenge to his medical skills that the Virginian's state of health presented him.

'Thought it was only during confinements that doctors called for lots of hot water,' Steele rasped through his gritted teeth, his lips drawn back in such a way that he showed an expression that might have been either a sardonic grin or a grimace.

'From what I can smell, I can guess near enough what I'm going to see after I've cut the clothes off you,' Beamish said evenly as he shifted his attention briefly to his bag and snapped open the catch. 'And I think that perhaps your reference to birth may prove to be somewhat apposite when I start to do what is necessary to treat your injury.'

'Going to get worse before it gets better, uh doc?'

'You are returned to good health or you die. No guarantee. But whatever the outcome, while I work toward it, you will certainly wish you had never been born.'

Julia reached the bottom of the hollow with a first armful of firewood, at the same time as Bart got there with a heavy cooking pot and his sister trailed him with two pails of water.

'No more humorous comments?' Beamish asked with a slight, tight smile as he produced a pair of scissors from his bag.

Steele squeezed out from his arid throat: 'Reckon I'll just leave a pregnant pause, doc.'

Three

THE DOCTOR, a look of eager concentration on his unattractive face, cut through the fabric of the sheepskin coat, then the jacket beneath, the shirt under the top clothes and finally the sweat dampened long johns to gain access to the wound. He worked quickly but deliberately with the well honed scissors and as he did so spoke evenly to his children and Julia French – instructing them where and how to build the fire with the cooking pot on top. His hands, which were as ruggedly formed and awkward looking as the rest of him, worked with delicacy and gentleness – so that after the sheepskin coat was cut and the two sides were folded back off the wound, Steele was no longer rigidly tense in anticipation of a sudden bolt of more intense pain because of some clumsy act by Beamish.

'That's fine, children,' the doctor said after a glance away from the wound to see that they had done as he demanded. 'Bart, you help Julia with the wood collecting now. And Arlene, get some bedding from the wagon so that we may make the patient a little more comfortable.'

The girl headed back up toward the Studebaker, still disappointed that Steele was alive and she could not have his horse. Her brother hurried up the other side of the hollow to go with Julia French into the timber. This as another wagon could be heard trundling along the trail.

'Ah, here come the Frenches with my good lady,' Beamish announced as he finished with the scissors. 'Getting to be quite crowded hereabouts, is it not?'

'Did you ever dig out a bullet before, doc?' Steele asked as the pain was briefly worse when the fabric of the long johns came free of the congealed blood and pus crusted on his flesh around the hole.

The fire under the pot crackled and spat and the water in the pot gave off a first wisp of steam. And the Virginian, aware that he was starting to get light headed again, had to concentrate very hard to retain a hold on reality – not to be conscious of the fire and water, and the future agony they promised, to the exclusion of all else that was happening around him.

'It wouldn't matter if I never had, Mr – ?'

'His name is Adam Steele, Dr Beamish,' Julia French supplied as she and the young boy returned to the bottom of the hollow with more wood.

'Thank you, Julia. My my, Mr Steele, you really have got yourself into a state by failing to have this wound attended to earlier.'

'This is all right, father?' Arlene asked.

'Fine, young lady. Some more water now, I think. Two more pailfuls should be sufficient. And have your mother come down here to assist me. Tell the Frenches they had better remain with the wagons if they are at all disturbed by the sight of blood and suchlike.'

'Some water to drink would be welcome, doc,' Steele rasped.

'I have some medicinal whiskey in my bag that I would rather you drank, Mr Steele. Water will serve to weaken its pain numbing effect.'

'I'm an abstainer.'

'Harriet, bring down some drinking water for the patient!' Beamish yelled, the raucous tone of his raised voice in utter contrast with the considerate gentleness of the way in which he lifted Steele's head and eased a pillow beneath it. From which new position, by rolling his eyes down to their fullest extent in the sockets, the Virginian was able to see the red and yellow fluids seeping up out of the ugly hole encircled by a scabby crust of darker colorations an inch or so above his right nipple.

'It helps any, Mr Steele, I've dealt with men in much worse conditions than you and not lost them. And to answer that question you asked a while back, I've removed bullets from tissue on more occasions than I can count – or would care to count. Probably did more amputations of assorted limbs and portions of limbs, but I wouldn't care to place a bet on that.'

'Delmar, stop living in the past and attend to easing the pain of this young man here and now. Your drink of water.'

'Mr Steele was in some doubt about my qualifications for treating him, Harriet my dear. I was merely on the point of informing him that I served as a surgeon during the war. With more time spent in the field than most of my kind who had the rank of major. Nick and Willa have no stomach for this, uh?'

'Grateful to you, ma'am,' the Virginian said to the woman who squatted down on her haunches beside him. And with one strong hand raised his head so that he could sip from the fine china cup she held to his lips with the other.

'It's little enough, Mr Steele. That and trying to ensure that Delmar does not enjoy himself to the extent of overlooking your suffering.'

She was close to sixty, which made her some ten years senior to her husband: and most unlikely to be the natural mother of Arlene and Bart. Very little taller than five feet, and with an amply fleshed frame she also bore no physical resemblance to the children in terms of her build. Likewise in her features, which were generously curved on the framework of a round face – large green eyes, a broad nose and a full lipped mouth above three or maybe even four chins. Her complexion was darkened from an outdoor life and the skin was marked with a myriad lines that were kept shallow only by the padding of fatty flesh beneath. It was a kindly face, but there was a suggestion in the green eyes that in combination with the redness of her short, tightly curled hair, this woman possessed a temper it would be dangerous to arouse.

She was attired in a serviceable grey denim dress and a wide brimmed once white hat that had an unstylish, homemade look about them.

She spoke as she held the cup steady, careful not to pour the warm but sweet tasting water too fast into Steele's mouth and throat. But spared the time to direct an indulgent smile at her husband – to ensure he did not take offence at what she said.

While he delved inside his medical bag, the doctor answered: 'When a man does not enjoy his work everything he does while he works becomes a chore. I'm sure Mr Adam Steele would not like to feel that in removing the bullet from him and treating the infection of the wound that I looked upon the tasks as mere onerous chores.'

'Enough?' Harriet Beamish asked as she withdrew the cup from Steele's lips.

'Grateful to you, ma'am,' the Virginian answered

and with moisture in his throat his voice did not rasp quite so much. 'For the water and the talk.' He was not able to move his head on the pillow: just his eyes along the sockets to shift his gaze from the fleshy, kindly face of the woman to the lean and ugly countenance of her husband. And was in time to see the man hastily alter his expression from a solemn scowl to a wry smile – as he finished with his bag for now and realised his patient was looking at him. 'Doc?'

'Perhaps you would see I have a constant supply of wetted swabs, Harriet my dear. Starting as soon as the water is reasonably hot. Yes, Mr Steele?'

The woman straightened up and moved around to the other side of the Virginian, to stand behind her squatting husband and beside Julia French who was absently tossing pieces of collected wood on to the crackling fire under the steaming pot.

'It would have got worse and then I'd have died for sure if your kids didn't find me. Now you're here, it's going to get worse and maybe I'll pull through. I've got nothing to lose except my dignity in front of a bunch of strangers. But I never did care much about what people thought of me. You don't have to look as if you're having fun, doc. But you go ahead and enjoy yourself. And don't mind me.'

It was the most he had said at one time since the children found him and the effort in combination with the tension of anticipating what he invited brought him close to exhaustion.

The two women and the man who listened to him each nodded at different times in agreement with what he said. And Delmar Beamish expressed professional interest centred entirely on the gruesome wound while his wife eyed Steele pityingly and Julia French looked away as she inserted a thumb and finger behind the lenses of her spectacles to rub at the tears that squeezed from her eyes. Then Harriet Beamish said:

'I think that any hotter will be too hot, dear.'

'Then we'll begin, dear,' her husband answered.

Julia French breathed a choked: 'Oh,' and kept her head pointedly turned away from the scene – peered up the sandy slope at where her parents stood with the Beamish children beside the stalled wagons.

The older woman stooped, picked up some tongs from the array of medical instruments and surgical tools Beamish had laid out on a cloth and expertly gripped a swab with them, dipped it in the steaming water and passed tongs and swab to her husband.

'Here you are, dear.'

'Thank you so much, dear.'

'And if I don't come out of this, thanks for trying, doc,' Steele said tensely, through teeth that were still gritted as he watched the sun glinting tongs move the water dripping swab toward him.

'As a qualified doctor of medicine I took an oath – ' Delmar Beamish started.

Speaking of oaths, I'm likely to sound off with a few and maybe the ladies should get back out of earshot, Steele had it in mind to say. But the first drip of hot water fell from the swab to splash directly into the infected wound. And it felt weightier and searingly hotter than it was. So that all the Virginian was able to do was squeeze his eyes tightly closed and press his teeth more tightly together between curled back lips – concentrating his entire consciousness on the fight against the impulse to give vocal response to the agony. An agony that was a moment later doubled and then re-doubled when the grim faced doctor lowered the swab on to the angry wound.

'Bastard!' Steele snarled, drawing the first syllable out to last for perhaps two seconds. And then hardly got the word finished in a whisper before his nervous system collapsed under this latest assault of pain and he was plunged into unconsciousness again.

Up beside the wagons on the trail, Arlene Beamish sighed and complained: 'If I hurt myself and hollered a cuss word like that while father was tending me, I'd have no candy ration for a week at least!'

She whirled away from the scene down in the hollow, an embittered scowl still contorting her tanned and freckled face as she moved along the trail, kicking angrily at a pebble.

'With all that candy the child has to eat, you'd think she'd have a sweeter disposition is my opinion,' Willa French murmured for just her husband to hear as she glanced disdainfully at the back of the small girl.

Mrs French was sixty years old, as thin as her daughter and with a face remarkably like that of Julia – except that the older woman's was stained and lined to the colour and texture of worn and neglected untreated leather. She had the same blue colour eyes, but her hair was thinner and shorter and was utterly white.

'Sure is hard to believe there's any sugar and spice in that one,' the just as elderly Nicholas French answered.

He was taller and broader with a face that was less ravaged by the passing of time. With a full head of black hair still, arced over a low brow above small grey eyes, a slightly crooked nose, sunken cheeks and a broad mouth adorned by a narrow moustache.

Both he and his wife were dressed in stylish, citified

clothing that was not suitable for trail riding and was showing signs of failure to stand up to hard wear.

'Hey, he's gone awful still, Arlene!' Bart Beamish called out to his sister as he peered fixedly down at the bottom of the hollow while his father worked with speedy deliberation to clean the old and festered wound with swab after swab handed to him with the tongs. 'Could be the horse is yours if Pa'll let you have her.'

He went to join Arlene in the game of pebble kicking out front of the lead wagon and weary team horses with a sorrel gelding hitched to the rear.

'Worse than snails and puppy dog tails in that,' French said grimly.

'After seeing those terrible children, Nick, it should make us even more grateful we were blessed to have such a fine daughter as Julia,' his wife countered. And smiled lovingly as she watched the bespectacled woman, on instructions from Delmar Beamish, move from the fire to kneel beside the injured man and grip his right arm at elbow and wrist.

Adam Steele opened his eyes, saw Julia French and felt himself aroused as he reflected on how good it would be to have the woman – but not as a daughter. Then he found the mere lustful thought totally exhausting and he went to sleep again. To surface the next time with the conviction that he had gone crazy. For Julia French appeared to have aged at least thirty years while he slept and that was just not possible – except in the kind of world created by a demented mind.

'Good morning, Mr Steele. I'm Willa French.'

'Ma'am, I'm real glad to hear that,' the Virginian answered.

'You are?'

'For a moment there, I thought you were Julia.'

'Gracious, it's only a week or so since we found you, young man. And Delmar took the bullet out of you. I'll go bring him now. He wanted to talk with you the first chance – '

'Too weak . . . ' Steele started.

'Not that long, young man,' Willa French corrected, before she realised she had misunderstood what the Virginian said and that he had slipped into sleep again.

Four

ADAM STEELE'S misunderstood comment was to prove prophetic when, two weeks to the day after the voices of Arlene and Bart Beamish acted to rouse him from the fringe of unconsciousness in the sandy hollow beside the trail, he came fully awake and remained so for more than a few disorientated seconds.

He was alone at the time he flicked open his eyelids, recalled much of what had happened to him up to the instant the hot water dripped on him, and felt a stiffness and soreness in the area of his upper right chest where the bullet had lodged and the infection had started. Alone in the rear of a wagon that was rolling slowly and smoothly over a flat and hardpacked surface that surely had to be a trail – and surely, too, the trail that had curved around the hollow at the foot of the timbered slope.

On the way down to the south of California right now, was how the fragile looking Julia French had explained the reason for the two wagons being on this trail when she was making small talk to try to keep from being sick at the stink of him. At a time when he was dying from a bullet wound he got to the south of where he was found. The bullet fired by one of many men who wanted to see him brought to justice for the murder of one of their own in Six Rivers County. Which was south of where he was found in the area of Golden Hill where he had escaped that community's rougher brand of justice. And escaped, too, the worse kind of death the miners and whores had left him to endure.

Joseph Mitchell had saved his life in Golden Hill. And the Beamishes and the Frenches had seen to it he did not die in agony in the sandy hollow. He had been helpless to take more than a token hand in his survival on those occasions. For which he could not be blamed, but it nonetheless went against the grain as he reflected upon his feebleness and impotency during the recent past. And now, from a present condition of mental alertness and marginally increased physical strength, he did not get irritated with himself for briefly dwelling on what had happened to him before he channelled his concentration into considering what the future could hold. For the half breed Apache from Golden Hill was directly responsible for the Virginian being wanted for murder in Six Rivers County. And, since this part of the country was so sparsely featured with communities and linking trails, it seemed to be a strong possibility that the Beamish and the French families who had saved his life were now unwittingly taking him toward a place where that life would be gravely endangered again.

'Howdy folks!' a man called, brightly cheerful. 'Welcome to town on such a fine day as it is.'

'Town?' Delmar Beamish countered in a sardonic tone.

The wagon in which Steele was riding rolled to a halt, behind the Studebaker from which the ugly and ungainly doctor had given his wry voiced reply.

'Gotta admit it ain't much, folks. But we got us the grocery and saloon and the church and the post office and the school to take care of the needs of everyone in the valley. And ain't no place in the county where there's this many buildin's all close together like they are. Outside of the county seat, of course. Fort Trinity that's called.'

Steele groaned: 'Sonofabitch!' and closed his eyes against the soft light of the wagon's interior, its level dictated by the filter effect of the grey burlap cover on the sunshine that gained direct access only through a narrow gap at the front.

Until the centre rear flap was jerked aside and Arlene Beamish admonished in her usual precocious manner: 'It seems that you only ever wake up to cuss, Mr Steele.' Then moderated her tone to add ingratiatingly: 'I been taking real good care of your horse while you're sick.'

She was riding the chestnut mare now, the horse hitched to the tailgate of what had to be the French wagon. Steele saw the head of the horse and that of the small girl through the flap Arlene held aside as he snapped open his eyes and jerked up his head – gritted his teeth and confined what could have been an obscenity to a low moan as the sudden movement erupted a bolt of sharp pain out of the stiff soreness at his upper right chest.

The expression was the kind that would likely accompany a bawling out and the girl gasped, released her grip on the flap of burlap and allowed the mare to drop back to the extent of the hitching line. While Adam Steele saw and felt that he was naked except for the stark white dressing on his wound under a just as clean sheet. On a makeshift bed of many thicknesses of blankets at one side of the wagon that was heavily laden with household effects.

He saw all this in a few seconds as he raised his head

from the folded blanket pillow, held it up for a moment, then thudded it back down again. And had the strength to do no more than roll his eyes to the upper limit in his sockets and see three faces in the gap that had now been opened at the front of the wagon's covering. Nicholas French to one side, Willa to the other and their daughter in the centre. Seen in an upside down image by the Virginian as they peered anxiously at him while Harriet Beamish joined in the exchange between her husband and the stranger – asking what kind of supplies were carried by the local grocery store.

'How you doin', son?' the moustached French asked.

'Do you know who we are, young man?' Willa posed.

'I bet you're feeling real hungry, Mr Steele?' Julia suggested, screwing her head hard to the side so that she was better able to see the Virginian, almost right way up.

'Weak as a new baby, sir,' Steele answered, returning his gaze to the burlap stretched between the bows immediately above his head. 'You are the French family, ma'am. And if I had an appetite when I woke up, Julia, I lost it fast.'

'Don't let that Beamish child bother you, young man,' Willa urged in a hushed whisper and with a scowl of disgust for Arlene. 'She is nothing more than a spoiled – '

'Now, Willa, I hardly think a man like Steele would be put out by a ten year old girl,' her husband cut in on her.

'It's almost noon, Mr Steele,' Julia explained eagerly with a smile in her voice. 'So nearly time for lunch. There's no restaurant in this strange little place we're in, but I promise that as soon as we get ourselves organised, I'll fix you the best lunch you ever ate.'

'After all the broth we been pourin' into you, son, reckon the toughest and stringiest piece of steak would likely taste of – '

'Pardon me, Mr French,' the Virginian interrupted.

'Sure, son.'

'Like I said, I'm not hungry so much. What I'd really like first of all is my clothes.'

He had been straining to hear the talk between the Beamishes and the local citizen against what the French family said to him. And had caught enough of it to know that the woman was satisfied she could replenish her larder adequately; while the doctor was not sure the community's grocery had all he required.

From the seat of the lead Studebaker, Delmar Beamish said: 'You see, we have a sick passenger, sir. I'm a doctor and the way I've had to keep applying fresh dressings to his wound, I've near run out. Going to have to make do and mend with bedding and clothing if the store doesn't stock regular bandages and – '

In competition for the Virginian's attention, Julia French said: 'I'm afraid you have none of your own clothes, Mr Steele. Those that the doctor did not need to cut to expose your injury were just too . . . well, too disgustingly filthy to do anything with. Except for your boots. We did not get rid of your boots.'

Steele rolled his eyes up in the sockets, intending to snarl his displeasure at the French family. But in time recalled that they were partially responsible for him not losing much more than a set of old clothes. And he confined his response to an even toned:

'Means my gloves and kerchief went, too?'

'Sentimental attachment, young man?' the older woman asked.

'Reckon it was time to change them, Mrs French. Had them a long time.'

'The knife in the sneaky boot sheath come from way back as well?' the man wanted to know and made it obvious he did not approve of the weapon and the way the Virginian carried it.

'That was kept along with your boots,' Julia assured. 'And everything that was on your horse, of course. Except for the food that had gone rotten.'

'Grateful to everybody. Everything was replaceable. My life isn't.'

'Proof of all else bein' renewable, son, is the way Julia here run you up some stuff.' Nicholas French explained. 'Undergarments and hose, couple of shirts and a pair of pants. Outta some of my clothes and some of the doc's. But seems to me it'll be a while before you're up and about and in need of threads.'

While Adam Steele was finding out about his clothing, Arlene Beamish had dismounted from the mare hitched to the rear of this wagon and run forward to report to her parents that the sick man was awake and not talking like he was out of his head any more. She interrupted her elders, but was listened to politely. Then along with her brother was granted the permission she demanded to go talk with the local children who were just breaking for lunch at the school house. After which, the local man began to question the Beamishes in a tone of voice far removed from the brightly cheerful one he had used before. And became irritably impatient when the doctor showed resentful reluctance to give direct answers to the probing queries.

'Wounded man you say?'

'That's right.'

'Accident?'

'No. He was found on the trail with a bullet in him. The wound infected with gangrene.'

'Far from here?'

'A good distance, sir. Several days travel. May I ask why you are so interested in my patient?'

'Way outta the valley, then?'

'This valley?'

'Yeah. This valley that starts up at the place where the Harlands used to live.'

'Delmar, that must have been the first empty house we reached,' Harriet Beamish put in.

'Where this trail you come in on got started, lady?' the local man supplied.

'That's right. The road we were on earlier ended at an old army fort that had fallen into ruin. It was rough going for two days before we reached the start of this trail at the empty house, wasn't it, Delmar.'

The doctor ignored his wife to ask of the local man: 'You did not answer my question, sir?'

'First house, at the end of the trail, is twenty-five miles from here, lady. Ten miles closer you rolled by another empty house.'

'Yes, we did.'

'Where Dolly Perry used to live.'

'Sir, I am beginning to be as intrigued as my husband by what this is all about,' Harriet Beamish said anxiously.

'This wounded man? Had a bullet in him here, did he?'

'Why, that is – ' the woman started.

'Harriet, until we have an explanation of – ' her

husband cut in.

'Avery, get on out here!' the local man interrupted Delmar Beamish. 'There's somebody aboard one of these rigs I figure you'll be interested to meet up with again.'

Nicholas and Willa French both turned around quickly on the wagon seat to see what was happening in the wake of the man's shouted words. While their daughter remained as she was, the burlap flap held aside so that she could watch the helpless and resigned Adam Steele as he lay on the blankets and under the sheet, awaiting the outcome of events beyond the confines of the dimly sunlit Studebaker interior: her lens magnified blue eyes expressing a mixture of anxiety and partial comprehension of only half understood situations.

'What's goin' on, Delmar?' her father demanded.

But there was no opportunity for the man aboard the lead wagon to respond before Willa French gasped: 'Nicholas, look there at the store. A man with a gun.'

'And a badge, too,' her husband pointed out.

This as Julia French looked briefly away from the interior of the wagon, but kept the flap drawn aside as she surveyed the scene to left and right. Then returned her now grim faced attention to Steele who continued to peer up at the burlap covering of the wagon as she said:

'You can expect no more help from us. But we didn't bring you here to this place on purpose. We didn't know you were in trouble here and that – '

'Don't none of you folks on the wagons make any move to resist what's happenin' here!' another local man ordered, speaking in a loud monotone, the sound of which mapped his progress for the unsighted Steele as he advanced on the French wagon from the front and right side. 'If the wounded man ain't the one that interests us, you'll get an apology and some good and fine Six Rivers County hospitality. If he is the one we want, you'll still get the hospitality after he's all locked up and . . . '

The man named Avery with the gun and the badge had reached the second of the two wagons, ambled along the side of it and swung around the rear. And Adam Steele was now able to add a family name to the given one, recognising the voice even before a much younger man called from the other side and the rear of the Studebaker:

'Hey, it sure looks like the horse that killer was ridin', Gramps.'

'You in the back of this wagon!' the father of Moses Jackson snarled. 'If you figure you got any chance of gettin' away – '

'He's not armed, sheriff,' Julia French said dully as she continued to gaze in at the Virginian, a brand of melancholic disappointment in her magnified eyes now.

While the faces of her parents who flanked her expressed deep shock while they constantly switched their attention from Steele to what was taking place at either side of their wagon and back again.

'And he has no strength to resist in any other way,' the bespectacled woman added. Then directed a sneering glance at the central gap in the burlap at the rear which was first parted by the barrel of a Winchester rifle, then held open wider by a gnarled, tanned and blue veined hand. So that a man in his sixties with a heavy black beard concealing his lower face was able to peer inside.

He said to the woman: 'I'm a deputy is all, ma'am,' as he stared fixedly at Steele.

'It's miss, deputy,' she snapped.

'Beg pardon, miss. Deputy Avery Jackson. Who is most appreciative of you folks deliverin' into his custody the man who murdered the last man to hold this office. Which was my son.'

'And my Pa!' a fresh faced youngster of about twenty added vehemently as he jerked at the other side of the burlap and wrenched it away so that he could have a clear view of the prostrated man in the rear of the wagon.

'And the Harland woman!' a female voice yelled.

'The widow Perry!' a man added harshly.

'Lloyd Weeks and Phil Tucker don't forget!' another man snarled.

'That's right!' another woman agreed bitterly. 'It's for killin' all them people the monster's gotta be tried and hung!'

'Oh goodness, did you do all that, Mr Steele?' Julia French asked in a strangled tone.

Her father swallowed hard and her mother gasped. Feet thudded heavily to the ground and Harriet Beamish urged:

'Take care, dear!'

The doctor's footfalls were almost as noisy as his impact with the hard packed street when he strode toward the French wagon and challenged: 'Adam Steele is my patient.'

'And my prisoner, doc,' Avery Jackson countered as the ugly, rough hewn face of Delmar Beamish showed at the rear of the Studebaker between that of the deputy and his grandson.

'Who as you can see is utterly incapable of resisting arrest, sir. So kindly allow me to supervise his transfer from the wagon to wherever you intend to incarcerate him.'

'Ain't no harm in allowin' the sawbones to do that, Gramps,' the younger Jackson said to the angrily undecided older one. 'Be a lousy deal if now we got our hands on the killer he was to kick the bucket before he could be strung up.'

There was a short pause before the deputy growled: 'Okay. He needs to be got over to the Flannerys' barn, doc. That's the frame buildin' just through the other side of town. Where the man with the rifle is standin'. You see it?'

'You see the place he means, Nick?' Beamish called through the wagon to the man on the driver's seat.

'Sure thing, Delmar.'

Beamish hauled himself up and over the top of the tailgate and instructed: 'Let's go then, my friend.'

'Inside with them, Jonas,' Avery Jackson ordered, and continued to hold the burlap flap aside so that his grandson could scramble unimpeded in the wake of the doctor.

It had been a day of lashing rain the first and the last time Steele had briefly seen the Jacksons, before the shots cracked out and he took the disabling bullet. It was the old man who blasted the lead into him and the Virginian saw that he had carried a vividly correct image of Avery in his memory – past sixty, black bearded, bright eyed, short and stockily built with a swagger in the way he made every move. Jonas he now saw as if for the first time. Lankily tall and thin with an emaciated looking face on which a mixture of fuzz and bristles grew, as fair as his neatly clipped and parted hair. He had large ears that protruded too much. And teeth like that, too. His eyes were the brightest blue and red rimmed with dark half circles of skin beneath them – as if he was an insommiac or did too much reading without the spectacles he needed.

Like his grandfather, he was dressed in a crisply white shirt, knife edge pressed black pants and an old and well used leather waist apron. Unlike the old timer, he had no five pointed silver star pinned to his breast pocket and he was unarmed.

He was eager to get into the rear of the wagon, then nervous when his grandfather let the flap fall closed and called:

'Okay, roll her over to the Flannery barn.'

The wagon jolted forward and the youngster tried to glare hatefully down at Steele. But was unable to hold the steadily returned gaze of the dark eyes and wrenched his head from side to side in an over anxious attempt to appear efficiently cautious.

'Don't neither of you two try nothin',' he warned.

And was ignored by the Virginian, drew a glance of disdain from the ugly awkward doctor who stood beside Jackson – the both of them hanging on to the overhead bow.

'You really killed all those people the deputy catalogued, Steele?' Beamish asked in a voice that had undertones of incredulity.

'No, doc.'

'Liar!' Jonas Jackson snapped.

Was ignored by both the older men this time.

'Killed one of the women who was on the point of killing me. Shot his Pa and a feller named Phil Tucker at about the same time as somebody else shot them. A joint effort, but I allowed the other feller to claim the kills.'

'Well, you admit you had a hand in the killin' a deputy, mister!' the youngster snapped with excited triumph in his voice and face. 'You tell that to the circuit judge down in Fort Trinity and it'll be enough to get you hung! And seein' you hung for what happened to Pa is all I wanna see!'

'Condemned man is entitled to a last request, kid.'

'Be a while before you get hung, mister! You'll be kept in the Flannery barn with the two guys that tried to rob Gramps's grocery until the sheriff gets here from Fort Trinity to take you back with him. Then it could take a couple of weeks or so before the circuit judge comes – '

'Won't ask for nothing else. Just some clothes.'

'We're there,' French announced from the seat at the front of the Studebaker.

'He has to be carried outta the wagon?' Avery Jackson asked as he used the rifle barrel again to hold aside the flap and look inside.

'He wants his clothes on, Gramps.'

'Gonna need to be dressed with ladies about, that's for sure. See to it and give a yell when it's done.' He withdrew from beyond the wagon's tailgate to ask of a man: 'How goes it, Dave? Prisoners behavin' themselves?'

'They sure are, Avery.'

The clothing which Julia French had altered to fit the Virginian was stacked in a neat pile at the head of his makeshift bed. Both the reluctant Beamish and the hostile Jackson had to help Steele don each garment, which immediately became limp and stained with sweat that squeezed from his every pore as he fought against the demanding urges either to cry aloud his pain or to surrender to unconsciousness. Then blood began to seep through the dressing on the wound to discolour the grey shirt.

'We got rid of all the poison in you, Steele,' the doctor said in response to the quizzical, pain filled glance the Virginian directed at him after he saw the crimson stain on the shirt front. 'And I figure you've made enough blood in the interim to replace much of what you lost. Nothing to worry about if you keep the wound free from further infection and don't lose too much more blood.'

'All ready, Gramps!' Jonas Jackson called, and extended a hand for the now sitting upright Steele to take.

The Virginian clasped the youngster's right hand with his left and nodded he was prepared to get to his feet when Beamish crouched to grip him under the left armpit and around the waist. Said through teeth gritted between drawn back lips while his eyes were tight shut and a bead of salt moisture stood out of every pore of his haggard face:

'Like the kid said, doc. Be a while before I get to the last drop.'

Five

THE VIRGINIAN in the reach-me-down clothing that had been altered to measurements taken while he was still losing weight, was unable to change anything about the grimace of agony that distorted his haggard and sweat run face until he was standing on the street, leaning against the tailgate of the wagon and kept upright by the strong grip of Delmar Beamish.

He felt able to crack open his eyes then, as Jonas Jackson backed off from him and he heard a chorus of subdued vocal sounds that was comprised of gasps of shock and various hisses of enmity. Too many softly spoken words competing to be heard for his pain punished mind to register any of them in comprehending isolation.

Yet he saw there were no more than a score of people arrayed in front of him as he raked his slightly out-of-focus gaze over them and the backdrop.

A backdrop of a small community in a broad, lush valley that ran in an arrow straight line from north to south within the limited confines of Steele's range of vision – seen in the way the early afternoon shadows were laid, truncated, to the front and slightly right as he faced back the way the Studebakers had come. The trail along which the two wagons had rolled followed a line close to the western extent of the valley's mile wide bottom land: running between the steep, thickly wooded slope and a band of tall grass sparsely featured with clumps of brush, stands of timber, rock outcrops and low knolls.

The building between which the wagons had first come to a halt were all of frame construction. Avery Jackson's Grocery Store and Saloon was a long, low building on the west side of the trail. And immediately facing this was the church, the post and telegraph office and the school house – all of these with a narrow frontage to the trail. These four buildings which the local people called a town were some fifty yards away from where Steele stood behind the French wagon, the Beamishes' Studebaker still parked among them.

The short and fat wife of the doctor was no longer up on the seat of the family wagon. Just as the Frenches were not aboard their rig any more – these familiar figures now mingled with the local citizenry in a loose knit group out front of the big barn with a rifle toting middle aged man who looked like a farmer standing guard on the double doors. Two other men in the now quiet audience had the look of farmers. A younger man wore the green eye vizor favoured by telegraphists, another had on the uniform cap of a postmaster and yet another the Virginian was certain taught school. The rest of the people watching him from close by were women.

He sensed that he was under surveillance from elsewhere and this puzzled him for stretched seconds until he recalled that the students at the school had been on the point of recessing for lunch. Now knew they had been herded back into the school house, from the windows and doorways of which they craned to peer between their elders for a sight of what was taking place outside Flannery's barn. Arlene and Bart

Beamish were nowhere to be seen.

'He sure don't look like no wholesale killer right now, Avery,' one of the farmers growled – his voice revealing he was the man who had welcomed the strangers to town.

'Looks a whole lot better than my boy when the posse found him, Willard,' the aged deputy countered.

'And he's still got his head on his shoulders, Willard Duff!' an ample bosomed, narrow waisted, dyed blonde haired woman of middle years added venomously. 'Not like poor Lloyd Weeks and that hussy the Widow Perry when he was through with them.'

'He says as how he only killed one woman and just helped to do away with Pa and Mr Tucker, Mrs Gruber,' Jonas Jackson said. And looked bewildered as he shook his head. 'Didn't say which of the women, though.'

'For the court to decide what took place when he's put on trial at Fort Trinity, boy!' his grandfather growled. 'Help the doc put him in the barn and save stuff like that for if you're called as a witness to the court.'

'I don't like to lay a hand on him, Gramps,' the youngster said in a whining tone and with a grimace twisting his mouth. 'He said right out in front of me that he put a bullet into Pa. It's like bein' a help to him, keepin' him on his feet and – '

'Hell, boy, helpin' him toward the gallows is all you'd be doin',' the darkly bearded deputy with the levelled from the hip Winchester rifle snapped. And thrust the gun at the school teacher to hold for him as he stepped forward.

But Steele made the first move, to step away from

the rear of the wagon and swing across in front of the much bigger built Delmar Beamish.

'You can manage, Steele?'

'Not without you holding on to me, doc.'

'You two men in the barn!' Avery Jackson roared, snatching back his rifle from the rotund, middle aged man with ink on his hands and chalk dust on his coat who seemed highly relieved to be rid of it.

'Yeah, old timer?' came a harsh toned reply.

'Stand back from the doors and don't try nothin' when they come open. Or Dave Gruber and me'll plug you for sure. No sweat and the court at Fort Trinity'll just have to deal with the murder case from the valley.'

He gestured with the Winchester for the thick set, clean shaven, sandy haired man who guarded the barn to open the double doors. And he did so nervously, awkwardly sliding a bar out of the brackets with one hand while he maintained a knuckle whitening grip on the frame of his single shot Springfield rifle with the other.

And Steele spent his time looking southward, alongside the French wagon and down the trail and valley that made a gradual curve to the east, the bottom land broadening and the flanking slopes becoming less steep. From the side of the barn to as far as it was possible to see before the curve of the valley blocked the sunlit view, the land to both left and right of the trail was either under cultivation, being rested as fallow or was fenced to keep grazing cattle and sheep from trampling nearby crops. Only the indigenous timber at the very tops of the valley sides had been left unfelled – with a very few exceptions lower down where a cluster of pines here or a spreading oak there had been allowed to grow on as shade trees in the yards of some of the half dozen farm houses that could be seen from town. Single storey, frame houses with low pitch roofs and stone chimneys. Built to a near uniform pattern, each with attendant barn or stable. Just one with a corral in which a bunch of horses was confined.

This was a good place, Steele reflected as he made his survey to the south, ignoring all that was being said and the actions it resulted in around him: confident that with Beamish's support he could remain upright and that the doctor would signal any move he was required to make. A good place to live and to work, to marry and to raise a family if that appealed to a man. A good place of unspoiled natural beauty to the north. And a good place that was rewarding careful tending by man to the south. With, dividing the two areas, the tiny hamlet that provided the valley people with their material and spiritual and educational needs. It was just such a place as this that Adam Steele had searched for in days long gone by, after he moderated his earlier aim to re-establish his lost birthright and would have been content to put down roots and run a homestead on much the same scale as the ones he could see from between the French wagon and Flannery's barn – until the door of the barn was swung wide by the nervous Dave Gruber and a larger part of what he had gazed at was blocked to his view. He would have been content, too, to have such people as those who watched him now as friends and neighbours – and had no doubt that he would, if the circumstances had been similar and all else were equal, have been as rancorously inclined toward a man in his position as they were toward him.

'Inside with him, doc!' Avery Jackson instructed, and gestured with his Winchester. 'That's it, you men, stay back like I told you and you won't get hurt.'

'Bullshit,' a man called sneeringly from within the shade of the barn's interior.

'Yeah, I reckon you're right, feller,' Steele muttered.

'What's that, Steele?' Beamish asked.

'Watch your mouth, Duval!' the elderly deputy snarled.

'You're the one that's talkin' the crap, lawman,' the prisoner with a harsh tone in his voice accused. 'Me and Eddie stayed back here because it suits us. Not on account of it's what you told us to do, lawman. So it's bullshit!'

Delmar Beamish moved slowly across the threshold of the barn, taking account of how much effort Steele had to expend on dragging one foot after the other.

'You said something?' the doctor asked, concentrating entirely on his frail patient as he steered and supported him with a hand under his armpit and an arm around his waist still.

While the Virginian peered directly ahead into the dimly sunlit, redolent aired barn – and managed to fix a grin to his sweat beaded, pale under the tan face that in such a low level of light was vaguely boyish. And said:

'Afternoon, fellers. Bullshit is right.'

'Uh?' the one named Eddie Duval grunted.

'Reckon I'm more like you two than any of those people outside.'

Bales of hay and some of straw had been pulled off neat stacks and scattered all over the floor of the barn. Maybe in anger, or perhaps the two prisoners liked to keep changing the position of where they sat. Beamish elected to steer the Virginian to such a hay bale to the left of the doorway – pushed it with a foot up close to the stack from which it had been taken and lowered his charge carefully down on to it, so that he could lean his back against the stack.

'I'm grateful, doc,' Steele said when he was seated, and his voice sounded to him as strange as it did when he was first fully awake in the sandy hollow two weeks ago. 'For everything.'

At these moments which seemed to him to drag by, elongated many times over, he felt an agony that was more excruciating than any he had ever experienced previously. Or so he was certain for what in truth was only a second or so. After which he realised he had been deluding himself. The hurt, which really was not that bad, was at least confined to the immediate area of the bullet wound. And he decided that what had caused him so much apparent physical agony was the mental anguish of being seen to be so helpless by such a large number of people. His damn pride was hurt again and in not being ready to admit to this, he had tried to pretend such a stupid and imaginary discomfort was caused by something else. Which was even more stupid. What had happened to him was not going to kill him, provided he took the kind of care of himself that the Beamishes and the Frenches had done while he was incapable. And in order to achieve that he had to work at facing up to the reality of his position. It was no time for pretence and self delusion.

In the darkness behind his closed eyelids – jet black shot with streaks of red that were the manifestation of pain and anger – he heard the thud of the big doctor's footfalls as Beamish withdrew from the barn. Then the scraping of the closing door, its impact at the closed position and the rattle of the securing bar along the brackets. Voices outside, speaking in tones of relief or triumph. A nervous laugh here and there. The voices diminishing and footfalls receding. One wagon moving nearby, then another further away but coming closer. Then both of them out on the south trail which ran along the curved, carefully husbanded section of the valley. Children began to shout and laugh and run and play.

'Welcome to the hicktown hoosegow, mister,' the harsh voiced prisoner greeted dully from where they both sat on bales at the rear of the barn. 'I'm Mal Davidson and this here is Eddie Duval. And you don't look to have nothin' in common with us, from what I seen.'

Steele opened his eyes and stared fixedly across the barn into which just a few stray shafts of bright sunlight penetrated through knot holes and small cracks between warped timbers. And focussed without blinking on a coil of rope that hung on a metal hook in a stout upright support of the loft. The coil of rope was about thirty feet distant from him and six feet up from the dirt floor. Kept fading out of sharp focus and sometimes seemed to contract in perspective as he struggled against frailty to stand up from the hay bale, shuffle to the side and then backwards until he could lean against the stack.

He had heard clearly what Davidson first said to him and had taken the speaking of the final word as a signal to start his attempt to rise. He thought that both his fellow prisoners said a great deal more to him as he strained and struggled, sweated and wept tears, groaned and cursed until he was up and back against the bales. And the coil of rope was in sharp focus at the actual distance again. When he said:

'If you said anything important while I was getting here, I missed it.'

'Not a thing,' Davidson growled.

'Hurts some, does it?' Duval asked.

The Virginian still did not trust himself to shift his concentrated attention away from the rope on the hook. But he was able to blink now without feeling he was on the brink of losing his balance.

'Some, feller,' he allowed, and thrust a foot tentatively forward, his hands still splayed on the prickly bales behind him. 'But that doesn't bother me so much.' Another step, with a cautiously slow movement of his hands away from the supporting wall of hay. 'It's being so weak that – '

'In the head as well as the limbs, seems to me,' Davidson said sneeringly. 'Way you're takin' all that exercise, a guy as sick as you look to be.'

Steele swayed a little during the first few steps but was never in serious danger of falling. Grinned his satisfaction but remained on guard against the danger of over confidence as he completed his walk to the loft support post with the hook and coil of rope. Reached it, grasped the hook and now turned his head to peer through the murky light of the barn's interior at the two men who made no effort to match his suddenly broader and more boyish grin.

'You want us to cheer or somethin'?' the harsh voiced, red headed, barrel chested, flabby bellied, fifty year old Mal Davidson posed wryly as he ran the back of a filthy hand over his mouth and spat the foul taste of it off his lips.

'First thing of any consequence I've done for myself

in the best part of three weeks, feller,' the Virginian said. And retained a hold on the hook as he turned around to face back the way he had come.

'Happy for you,' Duval muttered indifferently. 'One side of the damn barn to the other. Big deal.'

He was a head shorter than Davidson and so a match for Steele's height. About the Virginian's age, too. With thinning dark hair and a rodent like face – the eyes small and bright, the nose sharply pointed and the teeth slightly protruding.

They were both dressed Western style in dark shirts and pants, kerchiefs and Stetsons, and riding boots with spurs. Neither had shaved for a couple of days and maybe had not washed for longer than that – but the Virginian had his wits about him sufficiently now to be ready to admit that perhaps he smelled as bad as they looked like they might.

'And back again,' Davidson pointed out dully as Steele began the return trek: not needing to concentrate upon a fixed point this time.

'Every trip has to start someplace,' Steele said evenly to the two men who were eyeing him so disdainfully as he took each careful step and sweated like he was sprinting.

'Ain't no denyin' that,' Duval allowed. 'But you won't have to walk this trip, mister. The Fort Trinity sheriff's office has got this cage wagon for the likes of us to ride in.'

Steele reached the hay bale, turned and lowered himself slowly to sit upon it again. Sighed and smiled and then jutted out his bottom lip to direct a draught of cool air up over his sweat tacky face. Did some deep breathing for a few moments, then asked as he ran a shirt sleeved arm across his sticky forehead:

'You fellers reckon to take the ride in that wagon?'

'Sure don't,' Duval said.

And Davidson spoke quickly, as if he feared his partner was on the point of revealing an important secret. 'We got our own arrangements, mister.'

Steele nodded and got to his feet again – and started forward across the barn without first resting against the wall of hay bales.

'Tell you what, Mal.'

'Yeah, Eddie?'

'This guy keeps this up for long, the way he looks, be the local undertaker who'll be makin' arrangements for him.'

'Here, before they get the chance to get him to Fort Trinity and string him up, Eddie.'

'The man said gravely,' Steele muttered, and vented a short laugh.

'Uh?' Davidson grunted, bewildered.

Steele recognised the laughter as a sign of over confidence and struggled to spread a grim expression across his haggard, pale under the tan face as he looked at the two men at the rear of the barn and almost stumbled:

'Reckon I've been in a hole deeper than any grave-digger could ever sink, fellers. And I've had all the help I'm going to get to climb out of it, seems to me.' He reached the post, turned without grasping the hook, and grinned again as he said: 'God helps those that help themselves.'

'Uh?' Davidson grunted again, starting to get irritated by the Virginian's constant and uncharacteristic line of chatter.

'Needlepoint sampler that used to hang in the house

where I was born,' Steele explained as he once more set off across the barn.

'Then you ain't nothin' like Mal and me, mister!' Duval retorted and vented a short laugh. 'On account of we set more store by the sayin' that says the Devil looks after his own.'

'Far as I'm concerned, you can both go to hell!' Davidson snarled, and lifted his feet off the floor, to stretch out full length along some pushed together bales. 'Gonna have me some shuteye. Before your crazy talk drives me nuts!'

He tipped his Stetson forward over his face and placed his arms akimbo on his chest. Duval looked like a man who had been rebuked by a superior and fell silent – glowered down at the floor and sullenly ignored Steele. While the Virginian continued to walk and rest by turns: working the stiffness of inactivity out of his joints, coming to terms with a degree of discomfort that he realised would remain with him for some time and feeling a sense of determination to survive start to grow within him – despite knowing that there was a severe limitation to the extent he could recover physical strength in the present circumstances.

Maybe there was such a force as mind over matter. And with his life on the line, he had nothing to lose by putting the theory to a practical test. And with this thought firmly fixed in his mind, he sat down once more on the hay bale to rest. Remained seated for a long time now.

After a minute or so, during which the only sounds to disturb the peace of the dimly lit barn were the snores of Davidson and the happy cries of the children at play outside, Eddie Duval asked sourly:

'You all through actin' like a cat on hot bricks, mister?'

'For now, feller,' the Virginian answered evenly with another boyish grin spread across his emaciated, unhealthily pale face. 'Reckon for now I'll just be like the one that ate the cream.'

Six

THE AMPLY proportioned Mrs Gruber and another, less voluptuously built woman of similar middle age brought two trays bearing plates of food and mugs of coffee into the barn about an hour after Steele was locked up. The thick set Dave Gruber and the heavily bearded Avery Jackson flanked the open doorway with levelled rifles while the trays were set down just beyond the threshold – tacitly threatening that they were prepared to turn into actions the words the deputy had yelled before the bar was drawn from the brackets.

Not until the women had backed off into the sunlight outside of the barn did the thin bodied, hawk faced, mousy haired one say:

'I'm Rose Jackson.'

'What's that to us, woman?' Davidson asked as he swung his feet to the floor and folded up from where he had been sprawled out on the hay bales.

'Be polite, creep!' Gruber snapped and thrust his Springfield forward.

'Reckon you're talking to me, ma'am?' Steele said as he rose smoothly to his feet.

'Stay back!' Gruber blurted, and swung his rifle to aim it at the Virginian.

'One brave man I married,' his wife complained bitterly.

Gruber expressed a mixture of shame and anger.

Rose Jackson spoke before anyone else could. 'Moses was a fine man in a lot of ways. But not a good husband in one way?'

'That was a question, ma'am?' Steele asked.

'Let's get the doors closed up, Dave,' the elderly deputy urged.

'Was no coincidence, him and Phil Tucker and Lloyd Weeks bein' found dead along with the Widow Perry, was it? And Moses and Phil Tucker didn't just happen by the Harland place to find Emma and her Joan dead while they was out there huntin', I'm thinkin'?'

'Dammit, Rose!' her father-in-law snapped as he closed his door. 'That don't matter now. Whatever Moses and Phil was doin' out to the north of the valley, ain't nothin' that was more immoral than killin' folks.'

'I wouldn't know, ma'am,' Steele lied to the thin widow as Gruber closed his door and then the bar was slid.

The deputy continued to berate his son's wife and she began to weep. Mrs Gruber switched between comforting the woman and bawling out the man. Dave Gruber reminded Jackson that it was almost time for him to be relieved of the guard duty. Footfalls retreated from the front of the barn.

Within the barn, the three men moved to get their share of the food and coffee and returned to their former positions to consume the meal.

The school bell was rung, the children were assembled into ranks and roll call was made.

A man called Howard took over guarding the prisoners as the meal was finished and Davidson and Duval prepared to sleep off the drowsiness induced by the well cooked food and Steele recommenced his gentle exercise routine – but on a different route this time. Strolled from the front to the rear of the barn with no need to make any conscious effort at remaining on his feet, and able to take note of his surroundings in detail. Both within the barn and outside of it – the latter by peering through the eye level knot holes and cracks that admitted sunlight.

Within the unlikely prison there was nothing that offered inspiration for or aid to an escape. While outside, the prospects of making a getaway after breaking free of the barn did not look encouraging. In daylight, anyway. For the closest cover was Avery Jackson's grocery, some fifty yards to the north. To the west, in back of the barn, was a steep rise to thick timber on the crest: a hundred and fifty yards distant. Beyond the three buildings across the trail from the grocery it was more than a mile to where a man could find substantial cover behind an outcrop of rock – and a half mile further on to the fringe of the timber on the eastern slope of the valley. The first homestead to the south had its boundary marker just a few feet from the barn. But the house and outbuildings of the place were the best part of a mile down the trail, behind a yard on which the two Studebaker wagons were parked. There were open fields and an expansive meadow in between.

During frequent periods of rest, when he sat on the closest to hand bale, Steele formulated a number of plans which took account of all the variables he could think of and contained just the single constant – the taking of a hostage.

The afternoon lengthened and grew old. School finished for the day and the teacher with the ink stained hands harnessed two horses to a city trolley car converted for country use and drove south with the rig laden with children. Willard Duff took over from the man named Howard out front of the barn.

Eddie Duval woke himself up with a particularly raucous snore and spat forcefully as he rose into a seated posture. Growled:

'Boy, could I use a brew of beer.'

Steele, who was sitting much closer to his fellow prisoners than before, asked: 'Do you know when the sheriff from Trinity is scheduled to reach here, feller?'

'Don't know or care, mister.'

'The arrangements you and your buddy have to get – '

'Don't make allowances for springin' nobody else,' Davidson said from under his hat.

'Alone is how I usually prefer to do most things.'

'So why you askin' about our plans?'

'Wouldn't want to screw them up.'

'Big of you.'

'Or have you screw up mine because you were scared they would cause you problems.'

Davidson grunted and eased wearily up off his back, swinging his feet to the floor and putting the hat back squarely on his head. He did some more rubbing with the back of his hand and spitting with his mouth before he suggested:

'One way to be sure that don't happen, mister.'

'There is?'

'Don't do nothin' but act like the perfect prisoner of the hicks until after me and Eddie said our goodbyes.'

He rose to his feet and stretched, perhaps simply to ease the stiffness of a long sleep from his joints and with no thought at all of emphasising his powerful size.

'Shit, Mal, why don't you tell the guy the truth?' Duval said sourly, and drew a baleful glare from the bigger, older and meaner looking man.

'He ain't nothin' to us,' Davidson growled and dismissed Duval and Steele by placing his broad back to them and crossing directly to a crack in the south wall of the barn that was at his eye level. A vantage point he had obviously used before by the way he went straight to it and rested his raised hands comfortably to either side of the aperture as he peered at the outside world.

'Just 'cause he ain't so strong right now don't make him weak in the head, Eddie,' the rodent faced Duval rasped in a tone of complaint.

'Not like a guy that talks loud enough for the whole friggin' town to hear,' Davidson allowed, soft and angry, as he withdrew from the wall and spat without need to run a hand over his lips now as he turned to scowl at his partner. 'Town – some friggin' town!'

'You're the one started movin' around so I had to more or less yell at you,' Duval said defensively from where he continued to sit on the same hay bale as always.

And was ignored by Davidson who now sat on a bale closer to Steele and asked of the Virginian: 'I bet you think Eddie and me are a couple of real pikers? Hittin' the grocery in a hicksville place like this?'

Duval moved to a bale close to where the others sat, and lowered his rump on to it in time to add: 'And not only that, mister. To get ourselves collared for it.'

'None of my business,' Steele said.

'It was you started with the questions, Steele.'

'I told you why.'

'I know. And then Eddie here had to put his spoke

in. To make it sound like we're a couple of no account greenhorns who ain't got no idea how we're gonna get clear of this jam we're in right now.'

'That what he made it sound like?'

'Didn't he?'

'Ain't nothin' but the friggin, truth,' Duval murmured, and flinched back with a gasp of fear when Davidson spun round as if to lunge at him. But the top man of the partnership confined the venting of his anger to a rasping, inarticulate snarl and a glower across four feet of dimly sunlit, barn redolent space. Which encouraged the smaller man to add with a slightly challenging demeanour: 'Well, ain't it?'

Davidson looked even more ready to throw a punch at Duval now, but came down from the high point of anger quickly. Without a snarl and with a more vicious glare – but directed into the infinity of the middle distance between the group of three and the firmly closed doors. Then he sighed and allowed:

'Eddie and me are countin' on some help from our buddies, Steele. And they ain't the kinda guys to let their buddies down.'

'See we had this arrangement to all meet up here, mister,' Duval put in quickly, eager to be at the centre of attention. Shot a sidelong glance at Davidson, who showed him a yellow toothed sneer but left it at that. Duval obviously had difficulty in keeping his voice down, but managed it when he continued: 'Place like this was a good spot for us all to meet up, you know? Way out in the sticks, without no real law and with just a bunch of sodbusters and their families to get in the way of what we had in mind.'

'Have in mind, Eddie,' the scowling Davidson said sourly. 'Still ain't nothin' to keep us and the guys from doin' what we came here for. Which he don't have to know nothin' about.'

He jerked a thumb toward Steele, who made to shrug his shoulders, but checked the gesture before it could trigger fresh pain from his wound. Instead shook his head and answered:

'Your business is your business, feller. Right now, mine is limited to getting out of here. This barn and this county. I just wanted to be sure that if you had something similar in mind that we didn't conflict.'

'You know somethin', Steele?' Davidson said, puzzled. 'You don't talk and act like the sodbuster you're dressed up like.'

'I'm not, feller. Had a little trouble that dirtied up my clothes. A lady fixed me up with these. Talk the way I do because that's the way I am.'

Davidson nodded and showed a smile of quiet satisfaction, pleased to have been right about this aspect of the stranger.

'Mal and me were dumb to do what we done here, mister, and – '

'Eddie just talks, period,' the barrel chested man with the fat belly cut in, and spat at the floor between his feet. 'Ain't nothin' he likes better. Except killin'. We done our share of that, Steele. Just shoot people, though. Cuttin' off heads and stuff like that . . . well, we don't bother with it.'

Steele pursed his lips, then thrust out the lower one to direct cooling air up over his face. Said to the expectant Davidson and the eager to speak Duval:

'Reckon news of something as barbarous as that was bound to spread far and wide fast.'

'Eddie and me heard about it from the guys drinkin' at the grocery, mister. Soon as we got here the old timer with the badge was askin' us if we come across a guy looked like you on our way to town. Wouldn't tell us why. But the sodbusters and the clerks couldn't wait to talk about the killin's. You declare war on the people of this valley for some reason, mister?'

'No, feller.'

There was a short pause while the two fit men waited for the weakened one to amplify his reply. When he did not, it was Duval who looked ready to be angry. And Davidson who remained calm and said evenly:

'You heard what the grandson of the old timer deputy yelled, Eddie. That Steele claims just to have killed one of the women on his own. And helped out with the killin' of two of the guys?'

His tone and slight arching of his eyebrows added the query, which Steele elected to ignore. Davidson was irritated by this and Duval seemed to be pleased that his partner's approach had also failed to draw out the Virginian further than he wished to be drawn.

'Shit, what he done or didn't do don't make no odds to us, Mal,' the rodent featured man complained after another pause, and lowered his voice in response to a scowl by Davidson who also jerked a thumb toward the doorway with the guard beyond it. 'Fact is, we was plain dumb to take on so much liquor and make that trouble at the grocery. And the way I see it, it'll just serve us right if the guys make us kick our heels in the cage wagon from here to Trinity before they get us free.'

Anger expanded out of irritation and inscribed deep lines in the facial flesh of Mal Davidson as he snarled: 'If I find out them sonsofbitches didn't spring us first chance they had, I'll be kickin' somethin'! And it won't be my heels, Eddie!'

'Now if Steele here has got some kinda idea for bustin' outta this barn, Mal,' Duval said with a bright smile of expectation he shared between the two of them.

Davidson needed a longer period to ease out of his rage this time as he stared into the middle distance. And when, stretched seconds later, he did become calm, he looked about to dismiss his partner's suggestion with a sneer and a scornful taunt. Which Duval saw coming and checked when he added:

'It's gotta look better to the guys if we get outta here without no help from them, Mal! Ain't that so?'

The bigger, older man spat between his feet again. And kept his head bent, watching the saliva soak into the dirt, for a few more silent seconds. Then jerked up his head to direct a demanding glare at Steele as he said:

'Okay, what you got in mind?'

'Every meal brought to the barn the same way?'

'We was only collared and tossed in here this mornin', mister,' Duval answered. 'First chow we got was after you was tossed in with us.'

'Figure there ain't no other way they could do it that's better, Steele,' Davidson added. 'For them.'

'Yeah. So here's what I reckon we should do when supper's brought.'

He spoke in a rasping whisper and both his listeners leaned forward to catch every word, Eddie Duval expressing mounting excitement while Mal Davidson remained stone faced. It took less than a minute to explain and the rodent faced man seemed to have difficulty in containing himself for this long – when the Virginian was finished blurted:

'Hey, that'll work, mister. It'll damn well work.'

'Not without us to do the heavy work it won't,' Davidson put in sourly, directing another measure of contempt at his partner before he returned his gaze to the haggard face of Steele and accused: 'Which is pretty friggin' obvious. So all that crap about your plans screwing up ours was just that – crap.'

The Virginian executed a one shoulder shrug and answered: 'Not if you had something more in mind than sitting on your butts waiting for your buddies to spring you. In which case I would have had to think up something else. You're right in the other point you made, though. My plan won't work unless you do the hard labour.'

'Mal, it's for sure this guy can't do none of it,' Duval pointed out, passing back some of the scorn he had been taking. 'His state of lousy health.'

'Like it was said a while back, Eddie,' Davidson countered, gazing suspiciously at Steele, 'is he just sick from gettin' shot? Or is he maybe sick in the head as well?'

'What's that supposed to mean, Mal?'

'He's told us a way we can bust outta the barn, Eddie. But he ain't got us more than a couple of feet through the doorway. What's gonna happen then? We just gonna have to run like hell away from here? Carryin' him because he ain't in no fit state of health to run? And hope the people who hear the ruckus don't take it into their heads to come after us?'

'No,' the Virginian answered as Duval joined Davidson in eyeing him with quizzical suspicion. And now the rodent faced man started to grin again while Davidson's craggy face altered not at all. Until Steele had said: 'I reckon I know how we can get more than a couple of feet beyond the doorway of this barn. But if I told you about it in advance, maybe only two of us would make it.'

Now Davidson grinned, and nodded: sharing the expression and the gesture between his partner and the Virginian.

'Not sick in the head at all, uh?'

'Shit, Mal, he don't trust us!' Duval was bewildered and ready to be angry: with Steele as his target. 'Maybe you're right. Best we wait for the guys to show up and – '

'No, Eddie. Best we throw in our hands with Steele. And once we're outta this lousy barn we'll be free in more ways than one. We can go along with whatever else this guy has in mind. Or we can go our own way. Okay?'

'Hey, that's right,' Duval agreed, excitedly happy again.

'I was askin' you, Steele,' Davidson said, the harshness of his voice abruptly stressed as a hard light entered his dark, unblinking eyes.

'I have any option, feller?' the Virginian answered flatly.

'That's right. Now you told us what you have in mind to get us through the doorway, you ain't needed no more. Until we're outside. If then.'

'It's just when you're liquored up that you're stupid?' Steele posed.

The self satisfaction that had gradually taken command of Davidson's element burnished, dirt ingrained and heavily stubbled face was abruptly negated by an anger that was more rancorous than any he had felt earlier. But he seemed uncertain of where it should be directed – shared his burning gaze between Steele and Duval and the barn walls that blocked his view of the valley and its inhabitants. Then spat viciously at the dirt floor as he powered to his feet as a prelude to a possibly more violent act – that was checked by a light thud against the outside of the barn's south wall. A sound that caused all three men to snap their heads around, and Steele to vent a soft cry when the move awakened pain in his wound. And Arlene Beamish said in a singing tone:

'Salt, pepper, mustard, vinegar.' Each word spoken in the wake of a thud on the barn wall. The list of condiments repeated once more to the accompaniment of the four thuds before all three men in the dimly sunlit barn realised the small girl was bouncing a rubber ball off the timber as she played a lone game of catch.

'A kid,' Duval rasped on a sigh of relieved tension.

'Damn brat may've heard us,' Davidson hissed, and turned to head for his usual peep hole as the small girl continued with her game of catch but varied her sing-song recitation.

'Salt, pepper, mustard, vinegar, Bart's got a horse but I don't have one. Salt, pepper, mustard, vinegar, Bart's got a horse – '

'Hey, kid, get away from there!' Willard Duff yelled as he ran around from the front to the side of the barn. 'There's some dangerous desperadoes locked up inside of here.'

'Well, mister, I do not think that me bouncing my ball off of the wall will knock it down so they can escape,' the small girl argued, even toned. And began to thud her ball on the wall again.

'Kid, you just get away like I told you,' the farmer become a prison guard said to her sternly.

This against Arlene Beamish sing-songing to a different rhythm with the ball on the wall: 'You play ball with me and I'll play ball with you. Bart's got a horse and I don't have one.'

In an exasperated voice, Willard Duff snarled: 'Any kid from around here ignored an elder and she'd get her rear paddled by her Pa.'

Arlene quit with the ball bouncing and said in a condescending tone: 'Our father does not believe it is good for children to beat up on them, mister.'

While Steele remained impassive, in back of which he struggled to come to a decision on whether or not to shout at the girl to go to her parents and stay with them, Davidson became bored with the exchange and Duval grinned his enjoyment of the child getting the better of the man. Until a sound – a low scrape of wood on wood – drew the suddenly tense stares of all three to the doors: all of them instantly recognising the sliding of the bar along the brackets.

Davidson had been about to sit down again on the hay bale. But now checked the move and lunged forward – attempting to sprint with silent speed toward the doorway.

'Willard!' a man yelled fearfully from the area of the cluster of buildings to the north of the barn. 'What's that kid doin' messin' with the – '

'Shit!' Eddie Duval rasped through the grin become a scowl, as Mal Davidson pulled up short of the doors: three feet away from crashing into them as the bar was thudded back across the brackets to secure the entrance.

Steele murmured: 'Crazy kids.'

'Shoot, I wasn't doing nothing!' Bart Beamish complained from immediately out front of the barn as a man ran toward him from one direction and Duff rounded the corner in the other. 'Arlene and me were just playing!'

'That's right, that's just what we were doing, mister,' his sister augmented as she came to join the group beyond the doorway.

'Do it some place else!' the newcomer instructed. 'Here, loan me your rifle, Willard. Avery said I'm to relieve you.'

'Shoot, the grown ups around here sure are rotten to children,' Bart groaned as his footfalls and those of his sister could be heard on the south trail. While Willard Duff's heavier tread signalled his path as northward.

Davidson trod very softly for two paces so that he was up close to the doors and could put an eye to the crack where they met.

'Notice how you were scared to say shit around those grown ups,' Arlene pointed out to Bart from several yards off.

'I heard that, young lady!' the man on guard called, shocked. 'You should be ashamed.'

Davidson turned away from the doors and came silently back down the barn, a smile of quiet satisfaction spread across his face.

'And you should be ashamed to listen in on a person's private conversation!' Arlene countered in a high, shrill voice.

'Kids today!' the new guard said to himself.

'It's the telegraphman,' Davidson reported as he returned to sit on his hay bale, the smile still firmly fixed on his face. 'Holdin' that guy Duff's Winchester like he don't know which end it fires. And is scared it could go off without him doin' anythin'. With just the old timer deputy to worry about, it's gonna be a piece of cake. Let's get started, Eddie.'

He rose to his feet, and dragged the bale with ease from the floor up on to a shoulder. Duval was pensive as he imitated the other man's actions. Then paused to glance down at the seated Virginian and ask:

'You know them kids, mister?'

'Like I know this,' Steele answered, pensive himself as he reflected on whether he was pleased or otherwise over the outcome of the incident involving the Beamish children. There was an absentmindedness about the way in which he gently fingered the blood-stained area of his shirt front where it contoured the dressing on his wound.

'Uh?' Duval grunted.

'Steele means the brats are a pain, Eddie,' Davidson growled.

'Got you,' Duval said with a short laugh. 'But not in the chest, uh?'

Davidson sighed. 'Right, Eddie. What the brains there gets to keep sittin' on and what I'll start to kick if you don't move the one you got.'

'Yeah, yeah, Mal,' Duval said sourly as he went in the wake of his partner, matching his efforts to move silently. 'I get the message.'

'Keep it down, so the telegraphman don't, uh?'

The rodent faced man shot a long suffering glance at Steele, who murmured:

'Secrecy's the key, feller. Keep as quiet as a mouse.'

Seven

IT WAS evening, the sun down beyond the western ridge of the valley but with its afterglow still shedding a crimson light over the lush landscape, when three pairs of footfalls approached the barn from the direction of the nearest group of buildings. And the guard called:

'Supper's coming, you men. You step way back from the doorway, you hear?'

'Lead ain't what we want in our bellies, mister!' the harsh voiced Mal Davidson answered from midway down the barn, to where he had withdrawn when Eddie Duval – positioned at a peep hole in the north facing wall – signalled that Avery Jackson and the two women were on their way from the grocery.

Adam Steele was diagonally across the barn from Duval, closer to the front than the rear, not needing to stoop to peer with both eyes through a long and narrow split at the farm sectioned area of the valley. Where, here and there, the window of a farm house showed a yellow gleam of light. And where every chimney had for some time been releasing dark woodsmoke toward the cloudless sky as the men finished their toil in the fields and returned home for the evening meal. In all the time he had been at the vantage point, he had signalled just one event to Davidson and Duval before they became aware of it. This the return of the school teacher driving the converted trolley car now empty of children.

That had been an hour ago, when preparations inside the barn were completed and it was of no consequence that there was a vehicle rolling up the trail. But now there was another wagon on the same stretch of trail, and its presence could turn out to be of great consequence. To Dr Delmar Beamish and his wife who were up on the seat. To the four local people who were forming into a group immediately out front of the barn. And to the three men who were about to break out of the makeshift prison.

He turned from watching the approach of the wagon just as it rolled to within earshot of Davidson and Duval while the two men were taking long strides to get to the front of the barn before the doors were opened. They were level with him and close enough for him to see their scowls of vicious suspicion in the fast failing light of the almost gone dusk. Close enough for him to be able to rasp so that they could hear:

'Our transport. But don't hurt – '

He was unable to complete the instructions, as both his fellow prisoners nodded and wrenched their heads to face front in reaction to the shouted instruction of the elderly deputy:

'Any tricks and me and Ira Morrow'll start blastin'!'

'Just get the doors open so we can give the poor wretches their supper before they starve to death!' Mrs Gruber demanded. 'Why is it, Rose, that men that have the upper hand always have to crow about it so much?' She raised her voice to continue: 'I hope you people inside have the dirty dishes from earlier ready for us to . . . What on earth – '

Ira Morrow, his green eyeshade still in place, and

Deputy Sheriff Avery Jackson each pulled open a door of the barn after the older man with the black beard had slid the bar out of the brackets. At which moment the beefy shoulder of Mal Davidson and the less meaty one of Eddie Duval slammed into the wall of hay bales that had been stacked against the doors – stacked purposely without being keyed so that there was little resistance to the entire fifteen feet by twenty feet structure collapsing; to fall outwards under the powerful thrusts of the two men as soon as the support of the doors was taken away.

Jackson vented an obscenity and the telegraphman uttered a cry of alarm that was as shrill as those which came from the gaping mouths of Mrs Gruber and Rose Jackson. All four taken totally by surprise at the forceful explosion of hay bales. And unable to avoid being hit hard by the tumbling bales – as the men made a vain attempt to slam the doors closed while the women scrambled to get clear, hurling the cloth covered trays to the ground. The women and Avery Jackson were knocked down by the flying bales. Ira Morrow was bent double by a bale that thudded against his shoulders and neck. But he straightened up with a shriek of fear, pain and rage: to swing his rifle and his head in a desperate search for a target. But Davidson and Duval were both in the act of lunging out of the barn by then – and were unhampered by the shock that slowed the responses of the men they were intent upon disarming.

It was the bigger man who saw the danger of Morrow's action. And, too far off to have the time to make physical contact, Davidson heaved up a bale and hurled it at the telegraphman: with a roar of near pain at the effort he put into the attack. Which became a burst of triumphant laughter when he saw the tall and thin Morrow fold over backwards, his green eyeshade sent flying off his head, as the bale hit him end on in the chest. The rifle exploded a shot that tunnelled through a bale and into the dirt beneath. Though Duval was certain for a moment it was Davidson who stopped the bullet – the way his partner roared again as he did when he threw the bale. But the sound was a variation on the sound of triumph as the big man, sprawled out full length over fallen bales, got a one handed grip on the barrel of the Winchester: and was easily able to wrench it free of the shocked and partially stunned Ira Morrow.

When Duval snapped his head around to see the reason for Davidson's full throated bellow – and altered his expression from a frown of anxious curiosity to a broad grin that matched that on the features of his partner – the rodent faced man already had a rifle. The Winchester of Avery Jackson that had been much easier to win, for the elderly deputy had the wind knocked out of him as he crashed to the hard packed ground – hurled there by the opening of the door and then battered by the fall of heavy bales. So that the giggling Duval had only to stagger awkwardly through and over the scattered bales and stoop to snatch up the rifle from the vastly weakened grip of the bruised and struggling for breath old man.

Adam Steele was still on the threshold of the barn in back of the rubble like sprawl of bales: adding his raised voice to the bedlam of sound as the triumphant escapers vented their glee at gaining possession of the Winchesters. Also contributing to the din were the wails and screams of three women – Mrs Gruber who had tripped and fallen and was struggling to lift her ample weight up off the trail, Rose Jackson who was still running back toward the grocery and Harriet Beamish who was up on the seat of the Studebaker that her husband had reined to a halt a few feet short of where the hay bales had spewed across the trail out front of the barn. Delmar Beamish was yelling, too, at the snorting and rearing team horses that had been disturbed by the eruption of sound and movement and then brought close to panic by the crack of the rifle shot. Avery Jackson was groaning, Ira Morrow was cursing and a small group of people on the street between the grocery and the trio of facing buildings were shouting: apparently reluctant to make any move until the frantically fleeing Rose Jackson had answered their demands.

All of which meant that the Virginian had scant chance of having his warning heard by the Beamishes, who did not even spare a glance for him through the fast gathering darkness of night as the final crimson stain of the sun's setting faded from the western sky. The man too concerned with calming the frightened team while his wife was turned on the seat, shouting into the covered wagon.

At the kids to keep down and out of sight, Steele guessed as he roared: 'Give them their heads, you crazy fool! Get the hell out of here before – '

He realised that he was wasting his breath, as well as precious time and energy. That the Beamishes, although they were characteristically relatively calm at a time of dangerous crisis, were too concerned with what occupied them to be diverted. And they paid the price.

Davidson and Duval triggered their newly acquired Winchesters in unison and these shots – with their effect – acted to mute almost every other sound.

Davidson put a bullet at point blank range into the fear and rage contorted and discoloured face of Ira Morrow. To send the telegraphman back down to the ground from which he had half risen in a doomed attempt to regain the rifle – and managed to only loosely grasp the barrel as its muzzle cracked the bullet into him. The hay bales to either side of him quickly soaked up the great splash of blood that deluged them as the spasming nervous system of the dying man caused his head to be flung to the left, the right and then back again.

Harriet Beamish, shot over a longer range so that Eddie Duval's bullet did not exit from her torso, died with less loss of blood. The woman turned from shouting at the children, looked down at the small stain on the front of her unstylish gown, opened her mouth as if to say something to her husband and then toppled off the side of the wagon seat.

The twin reports drove the two horses in the wagon traces to a greater degree of panic, and Delmar Beamish may well have been unaware of his wife's death as he fought with reins and brake lever to prevent the animals bolting. Just the noise of the horse and the wagon, the snarling voice of the doctor and then the sounds of the two Winchesters having fresh shells jacked into their breeches as the expended cases were ejected could be heard in the wake of the killing shots. As Adam Steele suffered a torment of anguish that transcended all the physical agony he had endured during the run up to this tragedy he was helpless to prevent.

'Let's go, Eddie!' Davidson roared, and fired his rifle again, an instant before he sprinted forward: the chest of the unfeeling Ira Morrow acting in the same way as two hay bales – as resilient stepping stones before he reached the uncluttered area of trail beside the spooked horses. The animals briefly outside of a driver's control as Delmar Beamish released the reins and clutched at his throat – perhaps felt with his fingers the warmth of the spilling blood and the pulpy wound from which it spurted. But more likely did not, and was dead before his medical man's mind was even able to comprehend what had happened to him.

'So long, sucker!' Eddie Duval yelled and Steele sensed, before he saw, the need to tear his enraged attention away from the sight of the ugly ungainly doctor sprawling out across the wagon seat. Was in time by just part of a second to hurl himself with painful force at the rock hard ground: into the cover of two hay bales as the man with the face of a rodent swung his rifle and squeezed the trigger. To explode a bullet through the doorway of the barn. Where it dug splinters of wood from an inside wall instead of burrowing deep into the Virginian's already badly damaged chest.

The shouting and the screaming and the wailing had started up again as the wagon was dragged forward, two wheels locked by the firmly applied brake blocks. Davidson tossed his rifle on to the foot board, got a hold on the sluggishly moving wagon and hauled himself up and over a slow turning wheel – that would have crushed him had he misjudged the move and failed to get a secure hand hold. Then, with a sideways shove of his hip and a push with his hand as he sat down, he got rid of Delmar Beamish's body over the far side of the wagon seat. Kicked off the brake lever and roared:

'Move it, for frig sake, Eddie!'

Duval was clear of the scattered bales, still grinning his triumph at what he was sure was the killing shot he fired at Steele. And was about to trigger the Winchester again when he saw the wagon abruptly lunge out of the sluggish crawl into jolting speed – his intended victim the large bodied Mrs Gruber who sat splaylegged on the trail just a few feet away, shrieking foul mouthed abuse at him. But silencing the fat woman, ugly with vicious rage, was nowhere near as important as getting aboard the Studebaker that would speed away from these people who would likely tear him limb from limb if he got left behind. And he powered forward as Davidson steered the terrified horses into a turn away from the front of the barn. Then, like everyone else, the running man had his attention briefly captured by what looked like two loosely tied bundles that came out over the tailgate of the wagon and bounced and rolled through the billowing dust of its frenetic departure. Having hit the ground to either side of the sorrel gelding hitched to the wagon.

Eddie Duval, his fear of not getting aboard the wagon expanding by the split second, abandoned all thought of everything not connected with achieving his aim: and made a final spurt with both arms outstretched, the rifle still clutched in one hand. His free hand hooked over the top of the tailgate and he threw the rifle forward. It hit the tailgate and dropped to the ground, after first rapping him on a shin and almost tripping him. He thought he had no more energy left in reserve and that he was incapable even of drawing breath. But, like Adam Steele had proved to himself, so now this man did the same. Simply by wanting something badly enough, was able to overcome the seemingly impossible physical obstacles and get it – willed himself to take another breath, throw his trailing leg forward into another running step, hook a second hand over the top of the tailgate and then haul himself up off the ground and crash into the rear of the wagon. There to lay as close to death as he would ever get before his appointed time came.

Oblivious to the fact that Mal Davidson steered the recklessly galloping team into a complete turn and then was able to vent his pent up tension in a raucous laugh as he came close to taking his ease – needed only to maintain a light touch on the reins as the two horses raced along the straightaway and then the gentle curve of the trail to the south. Behind the speeding Studebaker, under the coating of gently settling dust kicked up by pumping hooves and spinning wheelrims, Delmar Beamish, Harriet Beamish and Ira Morrow remained slumped in the total and unmistakable inertia of death. Mrs Gruber sat with her fleshy legs still splayed, sobbing softly instead of spitting out obscenities now. Avery Jackson continued to lay face down among the scattered hay bales, groaning and shivering from head to toe as if he felt freezing cold in the only chilly night air. Rose Jackson remained, a lone and forlorn looking figure in the wedge of yellow lamplight from the open doorway of the grocery, peering in the wake of the group of men and women who were tentatively advancing on the scene of violence. The two Beamish children who had thrown themselves out of the rear of the wagon slowly sat up, bruised and in pain from their jolting impact with the ground but protected from serious injury by the suppleness of youth.

‘Shoot, Arlene, they shot our folks!’ Bart said bitterly after a glance at where his parents were slumped within ten feet of each other. There were tear runnels on both his freckled, breaking out with acne cheeks.

‘Shit’s okay to say in this kind of situation, Bart,’ his sister said grimly, dry eyed. But she trembled for a few moments before she could bring herself under control. Added: ‘And I don’t mean just because mother and father aren’t around any more to hear it. A person must relieve his feelings. Cry if you want.’

‘I don’t want to, but I got to!’ the boy complained tearfully.

Out along the trail, there was a single rifle shot as the Studebaker raced by the farmhouse and outbuildings where the Beamishes and the Frenches had spent the afternoon: and where the French wagon was still parked, without the team in the traces. Those who were looking to the south were able to see from the spurt of the muzzle flash that the shot was fired from the moving wagon at the farm buildings. There was no return of fire.

‘All because you want that chestnut mare, Arlene,’ Bart said with just a mild note of accusation as he ran a dusty shirt sleeve over his face to wipe off the tears.

The small girl turned from looking after the racing wagon and glared evilly at her brother for a moment before Willard Duff came to a breathless halt close by and asked with deep concern:

‘You two youngsters okay?’

‘Apart from just becoming orphans, Bart and I are fine, thank you,’ the girl answered with her usual composure.

The boy spilled more tears.

The man took his hat off and said in a chastened tone: 'I was meanin', are you hurt?'

'Bruised is all, mister. Thank you for your concern. But shouldn't you be getting after the men who made us orphans.'

The elderly farmer suddenly became aware that he was allowing himself to be taken to task by a child who deserved to be put over his knee and paddled for her attitude. But then he recalled she had just moments ago had her mother and father violently taken from her. And he could not release his anger – at the same time could not trust himself to keep it under control for long. Muttered: 'I'll have the women come see to you,' and backed away. Only then, as he spun around and jammed his hat back on his head, revealed the extent to which he had been discomfitted by Arlene Beamish.

There was a much greater degree of rage evident in the voice of Avery Jackson as, seated on a hay bale and surrounded by fellow citizens anxious for his welfare, he suddenly roared:

'What happened to the man who killed my boy? Steele weren't in no fit state to haul himself aboard that runaway rig!'

'One of them shot him, Gramps!' Jonas Jackson answered in high excitement, turning away from the group encircling his grandfather and pointing a shaking arm. 'He didn't even come outta the barn! I saw the little one – Duval – aim a shot at Steele!'

'Well go check it out, boy!' the elderly lawman ordered, his anger increased by the knowledge that Steele was possibly dead from a gunshot and so had cheated the hanging rope. And he rose to his feet and moved out of the press of concerned people, zigzagging unsteadily among the scattered bales to catch up with his grandson. Demanded of the boy who stood on the threshold of the barn, in the light of the newly risen moon peering into the darkness inside: 'Well?'

'I don't see him, Gramps!' the worried sounding younger Jackson answered.

'He ain't no dumbo like them two that took off on the wagon, boy,' the old timer said pensively after he had taken a few moments to compose himself out of the former anger. 'Be a waste of time and energy searchin' the damn barn because Steele's got more sense than to be hid in there.'

'I think I saw somebody on the hill in back of the barn, sir!' Arlene Beamish yelled.

'Good for you, girl!' the deputy roared. 'Let's us get a posse raised and go up the west ridge after him, boy. So he can be brought back and shipped to Trinity like we planned.'

'And them two crazy men killed poor Ira Morrow and the parents of them kids, Avery?' Mrs Gruber demanded. 'What of them?'

'They're fit and well and got themselves fast movin' transport, Emma,' Jackson reminded, scratching in his thick beard. 'Steele's sick and on foot. Be draggin' his ass real slow and so he's the best for the likes of us to get. Sheriff'll take care of – '

'And the fact you have a personal score to settle with Steele on account of Moses ain't neither here nor there, uh?' the amply proportioned woman said with a sneering tone.

'Now, dear,' her husband said to the woman. 'It's only sense, what Avery is sayin'.'

'Go to hell!' Emma Gruber snapped, and whirled to

hurry back toward the buildings that the local citizenry referred to as a town. And quickly overhauled another woman who was shepherding the Beamish children in the same direction.

Which left just the two Jacksons, Willard Duff, Dave Gruber, the schoolteacher, the postmaster and a pretty blonde haired young woman who held steadfastly to the postmaster's arm out front of the barn.

'All right, everyone here – exceptin' for Dora, of course – is deputised to ride in the posse,' the lawman announced officiously. 'That's plenty to find a man in Steele's state of health and bring him back. Dora, if nobody comes in from the country pretty soon to find out what all the ruckus has been about, want you to go bring in Wayne Flannery and have him attend to the dead.'

'But, Mr – '

'But me no buts, Dora Parrish. Let's go get our mounts, men!'

The group moved away from the bale littered area out front of the barn, the woman and the man who might have been either her father, husband or lover protesting that they agreed with Emma Gruber about the priorities of recapturing the escaped prisoners.

Until Avery Jackson curtailed their objections by snarling 'I'm the damn law around here and what I say goes, you hear! First comes Adam Steele!'

The Virginian, pressed hard against an inner wall of the barn, spoke in a rasping whisper through teeth still clenched in a grimace that was formed more by tension than pain or anger. Said: 'If what you say goes, feller, you were a little premature mentioning my name.' He eased away from the wall, and the grimace came close to being a grin as he looked along the length of the barn and through the wide open doorway. Said with less strain in his voice: 'Reckon it's only right I didn't get out with the others. Seeing as how I couldn't raise bale.'

Eight

THERE WAS no need to return to his token hiding place at the rear interior of the barn as the posse rode out of town a few minutes later. For the official deputy and the impressed men angled up the valley side in a direct line between their starting point out front of the grocery and the slight depression on the slope which was where the trees grew closest to the bottom land: thus did not pass by the open doorway.

Just as the sound of the hoofbeats of the posse's mounts, subdued by the lush turf of the valley side, faded from his earshot, the Virginian heard a wagon moving on the south trail. And used a knot hole close to where he sat on a bale to peer out at the brightly moonlit scene between Flannery's barn and the man's farm. Saw a buckboard approaching slowly with two people up on the seat and three more riding in the rear. Just dark silhouettes against the moon whitened trail. Next heard running footfalls coming along the trail from the other direction, and managed to get into hiding behind a stack of bales just before Dora Parrish came to a halt opposite the doorway.

While she waited for the buckboard to reach her, the pretty young blonde kept casting surreptitious and half afraid glances to the side. And for several moments the Virginian was tensely concerned that she sensed his presence just a few yards away in the darkness. But then he realised it was the stiffening corpse of Ira Morrow that she found so gruesomely fascinating.

When the buckboard rolled close enough so that she considered those aboard could hear her, the young woman made to shout. But only had time to suck in a deep breath before the voice of Julia French rang out, strident with shock.

'Oh, goodness, the doctor and Mrs Beamish! Mother, father, they're dead! Just lying there on the road for the carrion to come and devour them! These people here are – '

'Julia, Julia!' her father cut in on her in a patiently tolerant tone. 'Mr Flannery and his son are the undertakers hereabouts as well as running their farm. It was all explained. What were you doin' all the afternoon?'

'Wool gatherin' as usual, I suppose,' Willa French suggested in much the same manner as her husband as the buckboard came to a halt. And Steele chanced to look out from his hiding place as Dora Parrish began a fast and excited explanation of events. Saw that the tall and broadly built Nicholas French in his worse for wear city clothing was seated beside the driver who was a match for the other man's sixty-some age, with a slighter build, a thick and dark moustache that gave his face a grim look and a totally bald head which shone in the moonlight.

The thick lenses of Julia French's spectacles and their gold frames also glinted in the moonlight as the fragile looking woman got off the rear of the buckboard along with her white haired mother and a fat young man of a little over twenty who had the foolishly grinning and constantly twitching face of a mental defective.

'Howard and me,' Dora Parrish was saying, her rate

of speaking speeding up as she came toward the end of her account, 'we seen poor Ira usin' the telegraph machine plenty of times. So we was able to try to send a message to Trinity. But we couldn't raise no one there, Mr Flannery. And Avery Jackson figured them two that held up the grocery must've cut the wire some place out along the valley.'

'Real smart, our deputy sheriff,' the local farmer and undertaker growled sardonically.

'That's about it, I guess,' the blonde haired woman said. 'Only except that you should take care of the dead strangers and poor Ira. Avery Jackson told me to tell you.'

'Me and Sean will do that, Dora.'

'The children!' Willa French exclaimed. But not as a query. She was startled to see them suddenly – like everyone else out front of the barn, unaware of their approach until they arrived.

'Hello, Mr and Mrs French, and you, Julia,' Arlene Beamish greeted flatly. 'It's really awful about our Mother and Father being killed, isn't it?'

'You poor dears,' the white haired old lady said and began to weep the tears she had been holding back since she first saw the corpses of her former travelling companions.

'You want to come back to the post office with me, kids?' Dora Parrish suggested as Wayne Flannery and his son moved among the scattered bales to get to the corpse of Ira Morrow. 'Have some fresh made lemonade and some popcorn, maybe? While the Flannerys take care of what needs takin' care of?'

'Thank you, Mrs Parrish, but Bart and me would rather have something to occupy us to take our minds off what's happened,' Arlene answered in her arrogantly polite manner. 'Something more than eating and drinking, I mean.'

'Which is what we just been doing at the grocery with Mrs Jackson and Mrs Gruber,' Bart added.

'Just as you please,' the wife of the local postmaster said, and seemed pleased herself that she did not have to contend with the precocious and seemingly totally unfeeling children. Then turned and went hurriedly back to the huddle of buildings, as if she were afraid somebody might persuade them to change their minds.

Mrs French interrupted her quiet sobs with a sound that came close to being a retch as she saw the blood crusted face of the dead telegraphman. And forced out as her husband curved a comforting arm around her shoulders: 'I'm goin' to be sick to my stomach unless – '

She made the sound again, and brought up both her hands to cover her mouth.

'You folks want to go along to Avery Jackson's grocery?' Wayne Flannery suggested as he and Sean heaved the corpse on to the rear of the buckboard. 'I'm sure Rose'll be happy to sell Mrs French somethin' for what ails her. A medicine or some liquor or whatever.'

'We'll do that, all right, Willa?' French asked his wife.

'Please, Nicholas.'

'Will it be all right if Bart and I put the bales back in your barn, Mr Flannery?' Arlene asked.

'It's a chore has to be done,' the bald headed and grim faced man answered. 'But them bales could be a little heavy for you to handle, young lady.'

'I'll stay and help,' Julia French said. 'Guess I need

to do something to keep myself from dwelling on this terrible tragedy.'

'Sure, miss,' Flannery allowed and gestured for his son to help him pick up the body of Harriet Beamish.

'See they don't get into any mischief, Julia,' Nicholas French instructed as he shepherded his wife away from the barn. 'Guess we have to consider ourselves responsible for the children until something else can be sorted out.'

'We can be responsible for ourselves!' Bart muttered sullenly as he stooped to raise one end of a bale.

'But we won't be allowed to, while there's grown ups around,' his sister told him with calm resignation as she lifted the other end of the bale.

They carried it into the darkness of the barn, with Julia French in close attendance. And as they dropped their burden, breathing heavily from the exertion of the chore, the woman demanded in a rasping whisper:

'Well, I'm here with you. Now tell me what all that secret signalling was about?'

'Hush, Julia,' Arlene said in a warning tone. 'Wait until Mr Flannery and his crazy as a loon son have gone.'

'You shouldn't talk so about a poor, unfortunate –'

She broke off with a sound of exasperation as the Beamish children returned to the outside to get another bale.

'See, it ain't so heavy for us?' Bart called proudly.

'Worth a quarter to each of you if you stack them neat as I like them,' Wayne Flannery offered from the seat of the buckboard. And set the two horses in the traces moving. His son rode on the back of the wagon with the dead.

'Cheapskate sonofabitch,' Arlene rasped.

'Arlene Beamish!' Julia exclaimed, deeply shocked, as she stood on the threshold of the barn while the children struggled to bring in the second bale. 'I realise we must make allowances for you in the circumstances, but – '

The two children dropped the bale and the boy accused: 'You do go on so, Miss Julia,' as the girl stood on the bale and moved her feet so that she turned through a threequarter circle as the Flannery wagon rolled to a halt on the short street of the tiny community to the north.

'Really, Arlene, this is no time for – '

'For frigging around!' the small girl snapped. 'So come on out, Adam Steele. And let's get the hell out of this place and after the sonsofbitches that made Bart and me orphans!'

The Beamish children and Julia French heard the Virginian before they saw him. And Arlene and Bart grinned broadly as they peered into the darkness from which he emerged. While the woman caught her breath, then let it out in a long sigh when she saw him.

'Good evening, miss,' he greeted. 'You don't miss much, Arlene.'

'Oh, goodness,' Julia French exclaimed huskily.

'I miss having parents,' Arlene answered.

'And we'd like to see the killers that shot them dead as they are, sir,' Bart added.

'Your promise to try to do that – kill those sonsofbitches – is our price for helping you get away from these people,' his sister said gravely.

'It's ridiculous!' the woman blurted in a strangled tone. 'I just cannot believe any of this is happening.'

'It's happening,' Steele told her. 'You have yourselves a deal, kids. Far as I'm concerned. But Miss French seems – '

'Oh, you don't have to worry about Julia,' Arlene cut in, gravity abruptly replaced by her usual poised composure. 'We had to have another adult, in case you were still too sick to do any of the really heavy stuff that may need doing.'

'A man would have been best,' Bart put in.

'That's right,' his sister went on quickly, eager to reclaim the audience of two as she continued to stand on the hay bale. 'A man would've been a whole lot better – because he'd be stronger, you understand.'

'Of course,' Steele told her, trying without complete success to keep the tension out of his voice as valuable time slipped away.

'But there wasn't a man we could trust,' Bart explained.

'That's right. Whereas, we can trust Julia, we think. Because she's in love with you, we think.'

She giggled, suddenly a normal ten year old girl reacting like any other to an adult foible that to a child seemed totally foolish. Her brother was able to confine himself to a broad grin. While Julia French vented a strangled cry as she stared from the children to Steele and back again, her complexion vividly flushed by embarrassment.

'I've never been – ' she was able to blurt out before she felt compelled to turn her back to the man and the children as she tried to hide and control her feelings.

'And maybe you aren't now, Miss Julia,' the Virginian said evenly. 'But until you find out for sure, I'd be grateful if you would – '

'I did not intend to say I've never experienced love before, Mr Steele!' the woman cut in emphatically, her back still turned toward the Virginian and the small boy and girl. 'It's that I've never been so humiliated! And by children, at that!'

'Shoot, we better start hauling more bales, Arlene,' Bart muttered. 'In case they're watching and start to get suspicious because nothing's happening here.'

'That's right,' his sister snapped and jumped down from the bale. 'And before I throw up. Listening to grown ups talk that love and humiliation crap. Most – '

'Arlene Beamish!' the woman rasped, whirling to face the small girl.

Who stood her ground to finish: 'Most humiliating thing I can think of happening to a person is for him to have his neck stretched on a gallows!'

'Oh!' Julia French gasped, and brought her hands up to her mouth in the same way her mother had done a few minutes earlier.

The children stalked outside and there was childish anger in their actions as they began to bring in a third bale. The woman watched them until they were back across the threshold and then said bitterly:

'All right, I've come this far. I might just as well go all the way.'

She swept her lens magnified gaze from the children to Adam Steele: and saw that his smile was of deeply felt relief in contrast to theirs which expressed triumphant smugness. Then the Virginian pursed his lips to sigh and said:

'I wouldn't want you to do that unless you really loved me, Miss Julia.'

Nine

THE FRAGILE looking woman was in no mood to appreciate Steele's crude attempt at off colour humour. And the two children, forward as they were, did not have the worldly knowledge to understand what he meant.

He muttered contritely: 'Sorry,' and the apology went unacknowledged by anybody as Arlene Beamish began to speak quickly – while she and her brother went to work at bringing in two more bales.

'Bart and me have done our bit, mister. And you've been told what we want in return. Up to you now, with Miss Julia's help. There's nobody at the Flannery place right now. Horses in the stable there. For riding or for hitching to a wagon. The French's one in the yard or there's a buggy at the side of the house. Your rifle and the knife in the funny holster thing are under the seat of the French wagon. Guess that's about all. Bart and me'll keep on with this shifting of the bales while you two get the hell away from here.'

'And go get them men that killed our parents.'

'Those men, Bart.'

'What?'

'I always pay my debts,' Steele said as he went to the doorway, and leaned forward from the waist to peer northward along the trail. Saw that the buckboard, minus its freight of corpses, was parked in the wedge of light from the grocery. The horses in the traces were as unmoving as everything else in the vicinity of the one building facing three others. Under the gently wafting smoke from the chimneys of the grocery and the less brightly lit post and telegraph office. Now he checked the scene to the south and saw no smoke rising from the stacks of the scattered farmhouses and not a glimmer of lamplight.

From immediately beside him, Julia French said flatly: 'Mr Flannery told us that the valley people mind their own business for the most part. How, as the undertaker and the closest there is to a doctor between here and Fort Trinity, he had to come in response to the shooting trouble. Everyone out in that direction is probably in bed and asleep. Farming people don't keep late hours, as a rule.'

'And even the dumbest of deputies don't just ride around at night hoping to find a man who's left no sign, miss. You ready to go?'

'Yes.'

He went out the doorway and stayed close to the folded open door to reach the corner. Rounded this and halted to rake his gaze along the timber clad ridge and moon shadowed wooded slope below it on the west side of the valley.

'You're a long way from being fit,' she said.

'I know it,' he answered and started away from the barn, intending to head in a direct line from it to the farmhouse and outbuildings. Which would entail the climbing of three fences. And, because of the way the land rose and fell on the Flannery section of the valley, he and the woman would be in the cover of the barn – out of sight of anybody in town – for perhaps three quarters of the mile distance they had to travel on foot.

'You've lost some more blood.'

'I know it.'

'And the wound will open up again if you exert yourself over much.'

'Yes.'

'Horseback riding is out.'

'Uh uh.'

'So a wagon.'

'I think so.'

'Ours? I mean, my parents' wagon?'

'With you along, it won't be like stealing it. And the team horses.'

'When that strange deputy sheriff and the others get back, they won't have too much difficulty catching up with a wagon.'

Steele glanced back over a shoulder. Saw the Beamish children were still working steadily at clearing the bales off the trail to return them to the barn. He helped the woman over the first fence obstacle and then accepted assistance from her in getting between the strands of barbed wire that kept about fifty head of Texas Longhorns out of a field of winter barley. The cattle eyed the intruders from a distance, but the woman kept a firm grip on Steele's left arm: obviously nervous now there was no barrier between them and the animals.

'Never counted on help of any kind, Miss French,' the Virginian told her, constantly shifting the direction of his gaze to maintain a surveillance over the areas from which he and the woman could be spotted. 'After Davidson and Duval got the barn doors open. Didn't count on them giving me any more help and didn't have an idea in my head outside of a vague notion to make it up into the timber.'

He gestured with a hand toward the thickly wooded ridge which was now host to the posse hunting him. And as he lowered his hand, he was conscious for the first time how strange it felt to be without a glove – wondered if the fact that he could briefly reflect on such an insignificant side issue was a sign that his mind was beginning to function normally again.

'A vague notion?' the woman queried with more than just a hint of scorn in her voice. 'Was it also a vague notion that the Beamishes might possibly get killed in the process? A couple who had helped you when you were in desperate need once before?'

'I couldn't predict they would bring their wagon along the trail at just the time the escape was scheduled to happen, lady!' Steele rasped.

She caught her breath and shook her head violently as she blurted: 'Those monstrous children!' She looked hard at him as he continued to keep a constant watch over their surroundings. 'Could they have known what you and the other two men intended?'

Arlene and Bart Beamish were still at work with the bale clearing chore. The Longhorns moved without haste as they grazed on the far side of the pasture from where Steele and Julia French crossed it at a brisk but not hurried pace.

'The girl overheard us talking. When she and her brother tried to open up the doors this afternoon. For that the price was going to be just my horse. They were spotted.'

They were at the next three stranded barbed wire fence and something over half way to the Flannery farmhouse. Once more they took it in turns, each to help the other, get over and through the fence. Into a field that had been ploughed but not yet harrowed.

Which slowed their progress. And the woman held on to the man for a different reason now – worried he could trip in a deep furrow and open up the wound to erupt yet more fresh blood to moisten the ugly crust of that congealed on his shirt.

'It was no accident the Beamish wagon coming by at the time it did, Mr Steele,' Julia said at length, after they had both developed a gait that was awkward but nonetheless made crossing the deep ploughed field easier than if they had walked in a natural manner. 'We and Dr and Mrs Beamish were agreed to accept Mr Flannery's invitation and spend the night here. It would have been such a pleasure to spend a night in a real bed with a proper roof over our heads. But the children – particularly Arlene who I consider to be the most evil person of any age I ever came across – badgered their parents into moving on.

'Which did not require too much effort, since the Beamishes believe – believed in surrendering to every whim of those children. Which may pay dividends when they are adults, but I fail to see if anything will be worth such sacrificing of time and effort and even dignity that their parents . . . ' She sighed and then shrugged. 'But my opinion counts for nothing. And with the doctor and his wife dead, all that is immaterial. They gave in to the children once more and made preparations to leave. Came back this way first to purchase some supplies from the grocery. Goodness, I see it all had reason now.'

'Reason?'

They had reached a point, some four or five hundred yards from the cluster of farm buildings, beyond which they would be exposed to watching eyes in the community down the trail from the barn. The children had just three more bales to shift into the barn.

'Why they kept creating excuses to delay the departure they had been so keen to get started. They had to go to the privvy, Arlene had to say a final goodbye to your horse, Bart lost his hat.' She sighed and shrugged again. 'I can't believe those children comprehended the enormity of the risk they were running. For themselves and their parents. They had to consider it was a kind of game, wouldn't you say?'

A gate, hanging half open, gave exit from the ploughed field and on to the yard out front of Wayne Flannery's farmhouse. And relief at having attained the relative safety of the moon shadowed area between the house and the stable caused the sweat of tension and exertion to go suddenly cool on Steele's flesh. Initially a pleasant sensation, but then he felt weak and shivery.

'A game sure enough,' he answered. 'But I reckon they knew just how deadly it could turn out to be. Grateful if you'd hitch the team to your parents' wagon, Miss French. And tie my horse on at the rear. Bring my saddle and gear to the wagon if it isn't already aboard.'

She shivered, but in horror at the thought of the Beamish children. And set about doing as he had asked: handling the horses and the harnessing of them with a capable ease while never losing her look of fragility.

Steele maintained a watch on their surroundings and saw that just the small herd of Longhorns moved now, dark shadows on dark pasture. For all the scattered hay bales had been taken into the barn, the doors of which had been swung closed. Arlene and

Bart were nowhere to be seen. The Virginian was not idle as he looked for a first sign of discovery. He retrieved the Colt Hartford from under the seat of the Studebaker and unloaded the chambers to quickly test the action and check that the bullets were not corroded. Then he got the boot sheath and knife from the same stowage place where the rifle had been lodged and strapped the rig in place – used the needle sharp point of the blade to slice through nine inches of stitching of the outside seam of his right pants leg. Did not test his ability to draw the knife through this slit for fear of disturbing his wound. But was confident that after so many years of practice, he would be able to do it smoothly – albeit painfully – if the need should arise in the near future. When he first handled the rifle's rosewood stock and smooth metal barrel, and then gripped the knife, he was once more extremely conscious of the fact that he was missing the familiar gloves. And, with the knife strapped to his leg and the rifle canted to his shoulder he became aware that another item of his usual apparel was gone forever – raised an exploring hand tentatively to his throat and touched the age and element crinkled flesh where once the thuggee scarf had been draped.

Julia French saw this action as she finished the final chore of hitching the chestnut mare to the tailgate of the Studebaker and came to stand beside him. Said nervously:

'There is still a strong possibility that they'll noose a rope around there, Mr Steele.'

'Reckon so, Julia,' he agreed, and climbed up on to the seat of the wagon, favouring his right shoulder as much as he was able. Looked down at her to add: 'And the fact of you being a woman maybe won't count for much with them if they find out you helped me.'

'What do you mean, if they find out?' The moonlight glinting on the lenses of her spectacles acted to intensify the look of grim determination on the verge of anger that was spread on her fragile features. 'Perhaps the Beamish children will lie successfully about what has happened. But if they catch up with you, I'll be with you.' She raised a foot on to a wheel spoke and reached up to grip the handrail at the side of the seat. Then said: 'Kindly move over so that I may take the reins, Mr Steele.'

'Yes, ma'am,' he answered with a wry smile that was a match for his tone of voice as he did as she asked.

'South of course?'

'Yes, Julia.'

She released the brake and prepared to set the two horses moving. But first asked: 'Do you think I should drive fast or – '

'Just roll easy, Julia,' Steele told her and began again to cautiously survey his surroundings, paying particular attention to the areas from which trouble was most likely to come. 'And why don't you call me Adam?'

The darkly moon shadowed timber on the western ridge of the valley, the unlit Flannery's barn and the huddle of lamp lighted buildings beyond his former prison were all in the grip of a heavy silence that emphasised the total lack of activity within sight of the watchful Virginian. Even the horse in the traces of the stalled buckboard out front of the grocery and the small herd of cattle were silently unmoving – like they were party to some carefully laid plan designed to over-accentuate the slow and quiet progress of the lone wagon along the valley trail.

'I took no more care of you than I would of anybody in similar circumstances, Mr Steele,' she said out of the blue – and speaking just loudly enough so that he could hear her above the clop of hooves, rattle of wheels and creak of timbers.

'Sure, Julia.'

'For the three days at the place where we found you and then on the trail. Mother and Mrs Beamish took turns at attending to you during those first three days. But when we started to travel again and it was easiest to have you ride in our wagon, it was obvious that I would get to spend more time looking after you than anyone else.'

'Sure, Julia,' he said again.

She continued to peer directly ahead, as if for some reason she did not trust herself to even glance at him, as she went on: 'And it was perhaps inevitable that I should come to feel some kind of attachment to you, Mr Steele. You being so sick and helpless and needing me so much. And I guess those horrible children overheard me and mother talking. At a night camp a day or so before we got to this place. Well, I guess I've been doing a great deal of daydreaming recently, Mr Steele. About a man I used to know some years ago. Who used me and hurt me badly when he deserted me. And I felt I had to talk to my mother about him. And you. I can only think it was from eavesdropping on that talk that the children fastened on to the idea that I am in love with you. That and seeing me give you so much caring attention while you were sick. Which I would have given to anybody.'

They had started to swing from due south to south

east now on the long, gentle curve of the trail, and Steele could not any more lean to the side to look back and see the group of buildings beyond Flannery's barn. Now needed to look across the front of the woman at his side, waiting for the tiny community to come into view when the Studebaker reached the sharpest arc of the curve. Julia French misinterpreted the reason for his steady gaze and shot an indignant glance at him as she snapped:

'I suppose you think I am making a complete fool of myself.'

'No, Julia,' he answered, and leaned forward so that her head and upper body did not block his view of the distant town.

And the woman saw the frown that replaced impassiveness on his pale and emaciated face – turned to look at what had caused the change and uttered a small sound of shock. For the town, although it was as quiet as before, no longer gave an impression of being desolate in the moon and lamp lit night. For now a group of people had gathered on the area between the buckboard and the front of the grocery. Seen over a distance of more than two miles and each casting a shadow over the others so it was not possible for Steele and Julia French to recognise individuals. Three men and five women and no children.

'They're just standing and watching,' Julia said after a few seconds.

'So just keep the wagon moving like it is,' Steele told her.

'Why do you think they are acting that way, Mr Steele?'

'I don't know. Far as the local people are concerned, maybe they reckon it's the law's business and they aren't going to risk their necks by interfering. But if this was my wagon and you were my daughter, Julia . . . ?'

'My father is a peaceloving man, Mr Steele. But if needs be, he wouldn't be found wanting.'

Her lens magnified eyes challenged him to argue with this as she looked away from the silent and inactive group back around the curve of the trail.

'So he has good reason to do nothing right now, Julia. Which we can only guess at. And why waste the time?'

He began to peer in other directions again now, while she concentrated on the trail ahead. And they were as silent as their surroundings for perhaps a full minute, until the woman said grimly:

'Those children have something to do with it, I bet.'

'And I reckon you'd win, Julia,' Steele told her as she drove the wagon past another darkened and silent farm house.

'It's an odd feeling, isn't it?'

'What is, Julia?'

'That we are being manipulated by a pair of small children.'

'All you can do is try not to think about that. Which isn't very easy. Being hurt by the man a while back put you off all men, Julia?'

'For a year or so,' she answered without need to pause for thought. 'But then I began to allow gentlemen to call on me again.'

'But only gentlemen, uh?'

'What do you mean?'

'I'm the first killer you ever took a ride in the moonlight with?'

She did pause now. But to collect her thoughts

rather than to recollect distant memories. Eventually said: 'You talked a great deal at times when I was nursing you, Mr Steele. Most of it rambling nonsense. But I understood enough to realise you are a victim of circumstances. I know that you come from a rich family and that there have been few easy times since your father was murdered and you took the law into your own hands. You can't shock me by telling me anything about yourself, Mr Steele. Because I'm sure I've heard the worst of it. Which did more than just startle me when I was listening to it. But the way I see it, you are a man who has suffered to a greater extent than he has made others suffer for whatever the reason. And if I didn't believe that, I wouldn't be here with you now, for whatever the reason.'

'I didn't give away any dark secrets, Julia?'

'I don't think you have any, Mr Steele. Far as I'm concerned. You killed the Harland woman sure enough. But it was in self defence. But your half breed friend did away with the others, for equally good reasons, as far as you're concerned. Going to be difficult for you to get a fair hearing in a court of law though.'

'Like I got from you?'

'A man talking like you were does not lie, Mr Steele. But a court of law would not be much inclined to accept my re-telling of it.'

'You considered that?'

'Yes, I did. And I suppose I would have offered to testify on your behalf if you had been taken to the county seat by the sheriff and made to stand trial. Now, of course, after this has happened, I could not say a word on your behalf that would be given any credence. Since we are partners in crime.'

'Just in crime, Julia?'

'It is neither the time nor the place to consider anything not directly concerned with you escaping the gallows, Mr Steele.' For the first time since she had issued the tacit challenge for him to question the courage of her father, she looked at the Virginian seated beside her. And there was a different brand of gravity in her voice when she added: 'At least, anything so important to us as whether we are in love with each other. It will be much better for us to delay such a discussion until a more opportune time, don't you think?'

Because it was what he had been doing all the time, Steele was able to turn his head and peer up at the south western slopes of the valley without making it obvious he needed to avert his face in case his features revealed a response to what she said that would hurt her.

'Sure, Julia,' he agreed and to his own ears his voice sounded husky from the strain of trying to speak normally.

But the woman gave no sign that she detected anything was amiss – perhaps did not hear him too clearly because of the clattering made by the team and the wagon as it crossed a plank bridge spanning a stream. A stream that had its source in a stand of timber a half mile up the north eastern slope of the valley, made two sweeping curves on its downward way and then after crossing the trail followed it. Fifteen feet wide, flowing unhurriedly but crystal clear: bridged many times by planks to provide access to farm houses, fields and pastureland.

'Trouble should never come to a place like this, should it?' the woman said to end a lengthy vocal silence between them. And she sighed as she swept her gaze from one side of the peaceful and moonlit valley to the other. It was much wider now and the slopes had become less steep. The farms were more widely scattered and more of the natural features of the terrain had been let alone by the homesteaders who had plenty of usable acres without need of felling timber, blasting outcrops or levelling knolls. Here and there, other streams – none more than a yard or so wide and a few inches deep – meandered across the gentle inclines to join the valley's main watercourse. Sometimes bridged but more often forded where they spilled over the trail.

Steele had been watching the changing landscape of the valley for much longer than the woman – but looking for its potential dangers rather than at its beauty. He replied, in a tone far removed from that she had used, as they past the place where Davidson or Duval had cut the telegraph line:

'It wasn't my idea to come here, Julia.'

Ten

SOME TWO miles beyond the southernmost boundary fence of the final farm, the valley ceased to be and merged into an extensive, heavily wooded and ruggedly contoured plain. A mile further on down the less well used trail, Steele said they should pull the wagon off to the side and rest.

'You aren't feeling well?' the woman asked, very concerned, as she gently tugged on the reins to do as he suggested.

'I'm fine. But the horses have been hauling this rig for better than ten miles, I reckon. And ourselves and our complexes aren't the only freight aboard.'

The trail and stream had entered a wooded area at the side of a fifty feet high, sheer faced bluff. A ravine slanted down across the stream and trail from the east facing bluff and it was into this that the Virginian had the woman drive the Studebaker: and halt it in a patch of brush where it was concealed from the trail by intervening trees. Unless somebody had particular reason to peer hard into the ravine from this stretch of trail. And Steele climbed tentatively down off the wagon and went back to obliterate, as well as he was able, all sign that the wagon had rolled off the trail across from the bluff.

Nothing he did would have fooled an expert tracker intent upon finding his quarry. But the way in which Avery Jackson and his posse had headed off on a wild goose chase with not a single sign to follow indicated there was not an expert tracker in that group. While a bunch coming from the opposite direction – be it led by the sheriff from Fort Trinity or included Davidson and Duval in its number – would not have any reason to be searching for sign on the hard packed surface of the trail.

When he got back to the wagon in the ravine, the woman asked from inside:

'Did you expect to meet trouble back there, Mr Steele?'

'Sorry, Julia?' he countered absently after making a final survey of the screen of trees that almost completely hid them from the trail – and the trail from them. And briefly scowled at the gurgling of the stream running along the base of the bluff that would mask more distant and less pastoral sounds.

'You took your rifle with you.'

'Where I go, it goes,' he told her. 'Except when I'm in no condition to insist on having it that way.'

'Are you hungry?'

'I missed supper.'

'Me, too. The trouble started just as we were about to sit down at the table. I don't suppose we dare to light a fire?'

'That's right.'

'I haven't done anything about the horses,' she said to the accompaniment of the rattling crockery and eating utensils. 'You didn't say how long we'd be staying.'

'I'll see to it.'

'You're sure you can manage?'

Every movement of his torso caused some degree of feeling in the area of the wound; ranged from a twinge of discomfort to a bolt of pain that came close to needing a vocal outlet. But it was, at the time he undertook the chore, the most important task he could ever recall having to do – to take the two team horses from their traces and hitch them on a long line to the low branch of a tree. Because if he couldn't do something as simple as this – the kind of minor job he had done a thousand times before – he had no chance of ever escaping the fate that had threatened him from almost the first moment he set foot in Six Rivers County.

'Whatever complexes I might have, Mr Steele, I'd say you have a multiplicity more,' the woman greeted from the darkness of the wagon's interior: as the Virginian got aboard by way of a front wheel, the seat and the flap behind the seat. Choosing this route as easier than up and over the tailgate. But none the less breathing heavily and sweating profusely from the chore with the traces and this latest exertion. He was able to grin, though, as he experienced a sense of pride in achievement.

'I need to do things for myself, Julia. What do you need?'

'For you to eat this.' She, her eyes accustomed to the near pitch darkness in the rear of the wagon, waited until he had sat down: and reached across to set a plate on his lap. Then thrust a knife and spoon into the hand that was not fisted around the frame of the Colt Hartford. 'Which I fixed for you without expecting anything in return.'

He was wedged in the corner of the side of the wagon and the front. She was cross-legged in the area where he had ridden for so long on a bed of many blankets. He could not see if the blankets were still there.

'Just some cold cuts and salad I'm afraid I stole from the Flannery table. But I was meant to have some of it anyway.'

'You didn't there and you aren't here,' he said, his breathing becoming more natural and his flesh cooling.

'Don't worry, Mr Steele. I am making no sacrifice for you. I thought I was hungry, but then I found I just could not face the food. Everything has gone so wrong. I feel totally out of my depth, which is not exactly a new experience for me – but it's none the less disconcerting for that.'

'I reckon that applies to you and me both, Julia.'

'I know, but you can handle it, Mr Steele. You were right when you spoke of complexes, but I think I am loaded down with far more than you. You are your own man, temporarily needing to accept the help of others because you are sick. But you'll get better, Mr Steele. Why already you are starting to fend for yourself. I bet that if I was not here with you, to ask stupid questions, to fuss over you, to insist on doing my share of the chores and to keep on reminding you by my very presence that you are beholden to me . . . why, I bet you'd feel a whole lot better.'

Steele chewed the food carefully and swallowed it cautiously, unsure of how his stomach would react to a square meal after so long without solids. It tasted good going down and felt comfortable inside him. But he did not relish eating so much that he excluded what the woman was saying to him: while he also listened to the stream and the horses, hearing attuned to pick up any sound from outside the wagon not made by the water or the animals.

'There's nothing we can do to change what's happened, Julia,' he told her.

'I know that!' she snapped, then groaned in irritation at herself. 'I'm sorry, getting angry won't help. What's done is done, of course it is. And the way we are is the way we are. Some people can change. But not you, Adam Steele.'

'I'd be a liar if I said I thought I could, Julia. And a liar I'm not.'

'I've only told you the one.'

'About the gentlemen callers, I reckon.'

'Oh goodness, am I that totally transparent?'

'No, Julia. Just, like you said, out of your depth. The way I was when I was half conscious and rambling. And too weak to do more than just talk about getting out of the barn back there. It just isn't my style and it rankles. So if it helps, I understand, Julia.'

'You aren't at all like he was,' she said, softly and without haste, but starting to speak the moment he finished: so anxious was she to give way to the impulse before time had a chance to check it. 'Except in circumstances, after a fashion. But he was in need of help because he was penniless rather than sick. He was secretive and cunning, though. Set out from the very start to trick my parents and me, Mr Steele. Oh, dear.'

She sighed and it was almost a sob. But the weakening impulse was still strong enough to keep her talking. 'He cheated my parents out of money and me out of something which decent women are taught is beyond price. And in my shame, I shunned the company of men from that day to this. Clung to my parents with the conviction that I was to be a lifelong spinster. If not an old maid. It's not your fault, Mr Steele. I can't blame you for one single thing. From the start until this moment, you were either unable or disinclined to offer me any encouragement that my idiotic fantasies might come to something.'

Her voice had been getting softer and her tone more melancholic. And it was as if she only just managed to complete the final sentence before the energy required to speak was exhausted. But several stretched seconds of silence within the wagon elapsed before she began to weep. And a longer period of time passed before the Virginian said evenly:

'You're right, Julia.'

And she interrupted her sobbing with a sniff and countered: 'About what?'

'None of this being any of my fault. But that doesn't alter the fact that I owe you. You're going to have to help me again, though.'

'How do you mean?'

'Get yourself out of your own clothes and then me out of my pants. Usually, I take care of – '

'You . . . you monstrous . . . oh, what a fool – '

'Sorry, Julia?'

A scuffling sound accompanied her shocked exclamations, as she scrambled away from him. Going to the rear of the wagon.

'You're disgusting! To think that I meant I want you to . . . to do that to me! Why, it never crossed my mind to – '

'Julia,' he said against her stumbling protests of innocence that were getting increasingly shrill.

' – even for one moment consider you and I as no more than – '

'Julia!' he growled, his tone suddenly ominous enough for his voice to penetrate through her shock. And she became silent except for her fast and noisy breathing. 'You're shouting,' he went on, even toned now. 'And if the wrong people hear you, that could lead to something a whole lot worse than getting screwed for the second time in your life.'

She vented a squeal, like she had been physically hurt by his words.

'Lady,' the Virginian rasped as he heard a sound from beyond the confines of the wagon that cut across the trickling of the water and the cropping of equine teeth on grass.

'I prefer that *lady* to the way you have been calling me Julia, *Mr Steele*,' she whispered in a brittle tone. 'It is far more appropriate to – '

'Lend me one final hand.'

'What?'

Now she heard the sound that had captured his attention moments earlier and she uttered a strangled gasp. Then, peering along the wagon at him as he set aside his empty plate and took a two handed grip of the rifle, demanded in low, tense tones:

'I asked what you want me – '

'I said to lend me a hand, lady,' he growled. 'And I want you to put it where your mouth is.'

Eleven

A WAGON and horses were moving on the trail, from the south toward the north. One wagon, but many more horses than were needed to haul it.

The final gasp that Julia vented, in response to the latest insult from Adam Steele, was more than adequately masked by the gradually increasing body of sound as the group moving on the trail came closer to passing the concealed mouth of the ravine. Just as the noise the Virginian made in moving from the front to the rear of the Studebaker was covered.

The woman saw him coming toward her, but was too frightened by what caused his sudden move to be able to shift out of his path. So he had to go around her petrified form to get to a vantage point at the place where the two sides of the rear burlap met.

But she only seemed to be petrified – shuddered as he brushed against her. And despite the dangers of their situation, he spared one moment to hope that it was not the mere touch of his body against hers that triggered a reaction to revulsion within her.

Then, pleasing to him because he was at once able to ignore such an unimportant side issue again – a sign that there was no risk of his backsliding out of character now – he put all thoughts of Julia French and her problems out of his mind as he cracked open a gap between the two sides of the burlap and peered into the night.

There was little to be seen clearly, for very little moonlight penetrated to the floor of this timbered area: and the screen of intervening trees that kept the ravine as such a safe hiding place hampered his view still more. But with what he glimpsed, ill lit between the trunks of the pine trees allied with the sounds of hooves, rolling wheels, creaking timbers and saddle leathers, raucous voices and short bursts of harsh laughter, Steele was prepared to make an educated guess about the group passing on the trail.

Then he sensed eyes watching him. And hurriedly shifted his gaze away from the unsecretive group as the final rider moved out of sight. Grinned briefly at the threat of cold sweat that was withdrawn when he saw it was his chestnut mare on the lengthened hitching line that was eyeing him through the darkness of the night as the body of sound created by the riders and the wagon was muted by degree as they moved at a measured pace along the trail.

'It sounded like a whole army,' Julia French said in an awed whisper as Steele withdrew from the gap in the burlap. And turned, the tension draining out of him, to sit beside the woman with his back against the tailgate.

'Ten men riding horses and just the driver up on the seat of the Beamish wagon, Julia,' he reported. 'Maybe more inside, I couldn't see into the rear.'

'Goodness, they weren't just braggarts!' she murmured. 'Mother and father could be caught up in the trouble. We must warn people that – '

'Julia,' he cut in on her.

And she gasped again. 'Others are coming?' she asked, head cocked as she listened intently for a sound from outside to warn of more danger. But there were just those made by the stream and the horses.

'Ease your mind to be occupied?'

She nodded vigorously, could not be sure he could see this in the darkness and so augmented: 'Oh yes. But will we do something to warn – '

'We'll need the horses back in the traces. And a saddle on my mount in the event she's needed to ride.'

'I'll get right on it.'

She was in a scrambling hurry to leave the Studebaker. Went out over the tailgate, and before the burlap flaps came together behind her, Steele glimpsed across the top of her blonde hair that whiplashed with the near panicked speed of her actions, the actual cause of the threat of cold sweat that he had attributed to the mare. And he grinned again as he set about contributing something toward the chores of departure – manhandled his saddle and gear up off the bed of the wagon, over the top of the tailgate and let it fall heavily to the ground below. Then he went out of the Studebaker the same way: but lowered himself into the brush rather than dropped, so that his wound was not triggered to fresh pain by the jolt of a hard impact. It hurt enough from moving his saddle and gear. But it had hurt worse. And by remaining still while he waited for the woman to harness the team horses to the wagon, the discomfort was gradually eased. The wound felt wet, but it no longer burned when she came along the side of the Studebaker to attend to saddling the mare. Pale faced, but breathing heavily from exertion rather than over anxiety.

'You shouldn't have – ' she started, nodding toward the saddle, accoutrements and bedroll.

'There are many things I shouldn't have done, Julia,' he said, and moved away from the rear of the wagon to start ambling to and fro – with the rifle canted to his left shoulder, looked like a sloppily patrolling sentry. 'What I didn't do was take advantage of you and – '

'No man ever has or will since – '

'One of us will get to finish a sentence some time, Julia. Look, I'm sorry. I was trying to make some kind of stupid joke, I guess. To say you have the advantage over me.'

'What? I don't understand.'

He continued to amble back and forth while she saddled the mare. Steele working the muscles of his right shoulder from time to time to keep them from stiffening. The woman shooting quizzical and half fearful glances at him until he explained:

'When I was shut in the barn with Davidson and Duval, they started to talk about themselves and a bunch of others having something in mind for the valley community. I had no reason to find out what it was they meant. You spoke just now about braggarts and trouble which I reckon I may have reason to – '

'Oh yes, Mr Steele. Mr Flannery told us about it. While we were all having lunch after you'd been locked in the barn with those two. There, you want to check that the cinch is fixed right?'

She straightened up and backed away from the mare, running the back of a hand over her brow to wipe off beads of sweat. Glanced at the Virginian and then did a double take when she saw he was peering fixedly away from her – into the timber that almost totally screened the trail with the stream and the bluff beyond.

'Mr Steele?' she asked, half afraid again that he was sick and his mind had wandered.

'Hey, kid!' he called softly. 'You want to come over here and see that the saddle is cinched right to your horse.'

Arlene Beamish, whose presence he had first sensed after the riders and wagon passed by, then spotted as Julia French left the Studebaker, vented a squeal of excitement. Stepped into full view now and said breathlessly:

'You're kidding?'

'Goodness, however did the child get here?' the shocked woman demanded huskily.

'No I'm not, Arlene,' Steele told the small girl who came tentatively closer to the rear of the wagon, her freckled face expressing incredulity as her dark eyes shifted from the horse to the man and back again.

'But me taking the horse won't let you out of that promise you made me and Bart?' she posed, coming to a halt and her face starting to show a scowl.

'No, Arlene.'

'Arlene?' the woman hissed angrily as the small girl expressed a broad grin of pure pleasure and broke into a run toward the horse. 'I demand to know how you came to be here.'

'Hell, Miss Julia,' Arlene Beamish snorted through her grin as she patted the mare and pressed the side of her face against the animal's neck. 'From what I heard about you – a while ago and just now in the wagon – I figure you have to know there's nothing to that gooseberry bush crap.'

Twelve

TEN MINUTES later, when the wagon had been carefully reversed out of the ravine and was rolling along the trail – northward in the wake of the other Studebaker and its complement of escorts – Julia French broke her tight lipped silence to rasp:

'Violence is totally alien to my nature, Mr Steele. But I swear, if that child talks to me in that way ever again, I'll beat her so hard and long she won't be able to sit down for a month.'

This wagon had just the one escorting rider, who could not hear what was being said about her as she sat in the saddle of the big mare now hitched by a shorter line to the tailgate.

Steele, who had waited patiently for the woman to come down from the high point of her anger – speaking just an occasional terse instruction to her as the wagon was manoeuvred from the ravine – replied slowly:

'Can't claim to have the same opinion of violence you do, Julia. But I reckon I know how you feel about that experiment in child rearing that seems to have gone wrong.'

The Virginian waited patiently again through another tense silence. But this did not last very long. And there was less strain in the woman's voice when she said:

'I heard her talking to you at the rear while I was

getting this wagon back on the trail, Mr Steele. Did she give you any explanation of why we were not followed?'

'Seems she is supposed to be our hostage, Julia.'

'What?' The single word was spoken shrilly. But then, 'Oh, goodness,' emerged in a more controlled tone.

'Right, Julia. Those kids haven't just been pulling our strings to get what they want. The way the boy told it to the people in town you helped me to leave because you – '

'I can guess,' the woman said through clenched teeth.

'And we brought the girl with us against her will. Told the boy to tell people that if we were followed, we'd kill her.'

'Dear God in heaven.'

'While little miss smart ass came after us.'

'To give credence to their lies!'

'That, too.'

'What else?'

'Those kids are everything you think they are. And more. Especially her.' He jerked a thumb over his shoulder. 'But whatever kind of monster her parents made her into, that little girl loved them. And she's determined to see that the men who killed her mother and father get what's coming to them.'

'A man with your past can certainly understand that, Mr Steele,' Julia said acidly.

'Right.'

'Even in a ten year old girl who ought still to be playing with rag dolls instead of planning slaughter?'

'Seem to recall it was you wanted us to come back this way, Julia?'

'To get my parents away.'

'From what?'

'Oh God, I didn't tell you about that, did I?'

They were rolling off the plain and into the start of the low sided valley now: and Julia French suddenly altered her mood from frustrated anger with a problem that defied solution to anxiety over a dilemma which she had demanded the Virginian should solve. And her dismay was compounded by shame that she had forgotten about the plight of her parents while she indulged her chagrin for the Beamish children and Adam Steele's attitude toward them.

'No, Julia,' he answered, and rested a restraining hand on hers as she made to crack the reins and set the team to galloping. When she snapped her head around to stare accusingly at him, went on: 'I'm feeling more myself by the minute. And when I'm the way I should be, I try not to rush anything until I know what I'm getting into.'

She kept staring at him for a moment longer, then nodded and eased out of this fresh constriction of tension. Shifted her attention back to the trail and kept the team moving at a steady pace as she explained:

'It's one of these land grab situations, Mr Steele. We had some similar troubles up in Oregon. Though not on this scale. Or going back so far. Seems that this entire valley is claimed by an old mountain man named Orville Sleppin who has always maintained it was ceded to him by the Spanish when they withdrew from California. There were never any documents.

but never settled here and nobody ever took his claim seriously.

'A lot of claims were filed, and papers issued, back in the Gold Rush days. But gold was never found anywhere in the valley and the men who had claim papers were more than eager to sell out to Mr Jackson when he came through the valley and saw its potential as homesteading land. Oh, that's Avery Jackson, of course. This happened back in the early 'fifties, of course.'

'Sure, Julia.'

'Well, Avery Jackson was not a farmer or a rancher. Just a money maker who did not like to get his hands dirty. I am merely reporting what Mr Flannery told us over lunch?'

She glanced at Steele and he acknowledged what she said with a nod.

'At first he rented off sections of the valley to settlers and hardly ever visited here at all. Was off elsewhere engaged in other money making endeavours. But none of these ever amounted to anything and as time went by was forced to sell off each piece of valley land to the settlers who were working it. At good prices from their side, which is why nobody had any real bad feelings toward Avery Jackson.'

'Eventually the Jacksons were reduced to running the local grocery and saloon, Julia?' the Virginian prodded as the most southerly farm in the valley came into sight – a lamplit window of the house seeming to glint a warning of trouble in the dark early hours of the yet to be born new day.

'Yes. Avery Jackson had been widowed by then. Came to live in the valley with his son and daughter-in-law and grandson. Set up shop and everything seemed fine. Until Hal Sleppin – that's Orville's son – came into the valley about a year ago and tried to collect rent off everybody living here. Look, there's a light, Mr Steele.'

'I know, Julia.'

The woman thought she heard something in his tone that had not been there before and she shot another glance at him. But his pale, haggard, stubbled face had an impassive set that revealed nothing of what he was thinking. His two hands kept clenching and unclenching around the frame and barrel of the Colt Hartford that rested across his thighs.

'I've almost told it all,' she went on, quickening her tone. 'Hal Sleppin was either drunk or not entirely sane, the way Mr Flannery told it. And nobody took him seriously. But after he had gone, threatening to come back and bring men to help him get what he considered was his, Avery Jackson and his son went to Fort Trinity and had the son . . . '

'Moses,' Steele supplied.

'Yes, Moses. Had him appointed a deputy sheriff for the county. Well, nothing untoward happened until you and the half breed Indian were involved in those killings some weeks ago, Mr Steele. When people thought you two might have been part of some group paid by the younger Sleppin to implement his threats.'

She peered hard into his uncommunicative profile again – as if it only now occurred to her to consider such a possibility. Steele did not return her gaze, but revealed he was aware of her scrutiny – allowed just a second to pass before he said:

'I can see how they might have thought that, Julia.

And it explains how old man Jackson was able to keep the posse coming after Joseph Mitchell and me for so long.'

She nodded as she returned her attention to the trail as she drove the wagon by the plank bridge entrance to the farm with a light shafting away from it – no longer an ominous gleam in the night at such close quarters. Instead, a pale finger of light fallen from the open doorway: angled partially at the trail and also in the general direction of the way in which the owner of the place had gone. Or been taken? Owner and his family? There had been no explosive sounds of violence and nothing about the quiet farmstead with the open door that suggested any force had been used here. Just an emanation in the steady glow of the lamplight of melancholic desolation.

'He hasn't been popular hereabouts since the question of ownership was raised, Mr Steele,' Julia French went on after the meagrely illuminated farm was behind them. And another place, unlit, could be seen in the distance on the other side of the trail. 'The family rallied round Mr Jackson and so they were all treated much the same. By almost everybody except a few of the closer neighbours.'

'Gathered that, Julia. Did Davidson or Duval do or say anything to make matters worse?'

'Well, it appears they just rode into the valley from this direction, making themselves objectionable to everyone they met along the trail. Drunk and laughing and using obscene language and such like. And threatening people that they would do well to leave their places. Then, at Mr Jackson's grocery, they brought fresh liquor and became more objectionable. Warned that the whole valley would be put to the torch when their friends got here. When they wanted more liquor, Mr Jackson refused to sell it to them and that's when they pulled out their guns and held up the place. But they were so drunk, Mr Jackson and his grandson were easily able to disarm them.'

'Didn't strike me as being examples of the best there are available,' Steele murmured softly, and began to flex his punished chest and shoulder muscles again.

'The best?' Julia countered, puzzled.

'Gunslingers, heavies, troublemakers, people-pushers. . . whatever it was Hal Sleppin had in mind to take care of what he reckons to be his business hereabouts. Guess he's not a rich man without the valley properties?'

'A no account, broken down drifter is how Mr Flannery described the man, as I recall,' Julia answered. 'But I think it would be wrong to dismiss such a large group of men with guns with insulting words, Mr Steele.'

'Sure, Julia,' he agreed as the wagon rolled by the second abandoned farm. 'Like the lady riding my horse might say, sticks and stones can break their bones – '

'But names will never hurt them,' the freckle faced small girl with views far beyond her years completed as she brought the chestnut mare up alongside the front end of the Studebaker. 'Whose horse did you say, mister?'

She rode on the offside of the wagon, next to the woman who was turned to peer at the farmstead in search of life so that she blocked the litte girl's view of Steele. And thus the Virginian's brief scowl at being taken to task by a child of ten went unseen.

'Slip of the tongue,' he said lamely.

'Whatever those men are or are not, Mr Steele,' Julia said anxiously, 'they appear to have exerted considerable influence over the people who live – '

'Killed them maybe,' Arlene Beamish cut in offhandedly. 'Got bored with just riding my new horse while she was hitched to the wagon. And figured that since she's mine, I can do as I like with her. Can't wait to show Bart she's mine now. See you later, Miss Julia, mister!'

She yelled the farewell as she thudded in her heels to set the mare into a gallop: and the sound of the pumping hooves on the hard packed trail was like thunder in contrast to the regular and less frenetic sounds that had previously disturbed the tranquillity of the valley in the cold early hours.

Julia French, spectacle frames and lenses reflecting the light of the moon with every jerky motion of her head, was suffering another shock of realisation as she shifted her gaze constantly between the nearby farm, two more that could be seen along the trail and the galloping horse with the small girl riding it.

'Perhaps she's right about the people from the farms, Mr Steele,' the woman rasped as the beat of hooves receded into the distance.

'Ten year old girls can be wrong sometimes, Julia,' the Virginian answered, impassive again after controlling the emotion that had fastened an almost painful grip on him while he watched Arlene Beamish ride away. A white hot fury that was seen in the form of a vicious grimace on his sickness ravaged features – and came near to finding an outlet in the action of bringing his rifle to the aim and squeezing the trigger. 'If there were new dead in those farmhouses, I'd know it.'

She heard the after-effects of the strain of self control in his tone and now looked hard at him: as he continued to gaze up ths trail after the child and the horse.

'But how could you?' she asked, then answered the question herself as he pursed his lips prior to replying. 'You'd just know. Death and you . . . '

She didn't know how to finish what she had started: or was too afraid to complete what she had in mind. Perturbed even to be in the company of Adam Steele in this new mood that had gripped him.

'What about Arlene?' she asked after several seconds had passed and he had made no attempt to confirm or deny her opinion.

The hooves of the team horses and then the wheel-rims of the wagon rattled on the planking of the first bridge they had crossed on the way south. At the point where the stream running down the north eastern slope of the valley cut across the trail. The horse and its young rider were out of sight now, but Julia French none the less suffered another shock that caused her to catch her breath as she snapped her head around to search for Arlene Beamish. This as, seemingly in response to her query, Steele raised the Colt Hartford up from his lap. But he gestured with the rifle rather than aimed it – and indicated the south western slope of the valley. Pointing across the fields and pastures of two farms which were spread along the start of the valley's curve around which the chestnut mare had already carried the small girl.

'Like you to drive the wagon up to the timber on the ridge, Julia.'

She headed the team off the trail and on to an area of lush grazing land through an open gateway:

followed his instruction at once and needed to pay attention to the turn for just a few seconds before she reverted her intent gaze to the stone like profile of Adam Steele to insist:

'I asked you what about that child?'

'Sorry, Julia. Too much else on my mind. Don't have the time to be concerned about a minor problem.'

Thirteen

THE VIRGINIAN had miscounted by one the number of men who had ridden past the mouth of the ravine by the bluff beyond the southern end of the valley. There were twelve of them, not eleven. But he did not think he had miscalculated in his estimation of the kind of men they were. Each was as different from the other in age and physical appearance and intelligence as was Mal Davidson from Eddie Duval. But, like these two former fellow prisoners of Adam Steele in Flannery's barn – who were numbered among the twelve – they all shared a common factor. Causing trouble was their business and they enjoyed their work.

At sun up in the beautiful valley's tiny commercial centre, Hal Sleppin and his men were having a lot of fun – at the expense of upwards of fifty men, women and children.

The farmers and their families were all hurriedly dressed, unshaven and dishevelled, red eyed from having their rest interrupted and variously suffered consternation, dismay and fretfulness as they stood in a closeknit group on the trail between Flannery's barn and the huddle of buildings dominated by Avery Jackson's grocery. Like a tightly run herd of cattle, skittish but quiet under the scrutiny of the confidently smiling men who sat their easy standing horses in an uneven arc between Flannery's barn and the crowd.

Some with rifles drawn from the boot but aimed negligently skywards. Others with hands draped over the butts of holstered revolvers. A few not feeling it was yet necessary to touch their guns. Eleven horsemen.

The twelfth man was still up on the seat of the Beamish Studebaker, which was parked off the trail at the side of the crowd, the weary team still in the traces. And Bart Beamish's sorrel gelding hitched to the rear still.

'Okay, Sleppin!' Avery Jackson shouted from within his grocery. 'You and them other creeps you brought along all through treatin' people like critters? You wanna use your mouth some more?'

There had been a shouted exchange by turns of angry and taunting words while Adam Steele and Julia French rode the wagon closer to the tense centre of what seemed set to be a scene of violence. But there had been too much noise of movement and other voices for the sense of what was being yelled back and forth to reach the ears of the couple who made covert progress aboard the wagon through the timber on the ridge above and to the west of their objective. But it was a body of sound that served their purpose well – masked the lesser noise made by their one wagon and two horses.

Tall and thin, perhaps fifty years old although it was difficult to tell through the grimed in dirt and straggly brown beard that stained and concealed much of his lean face, Sleppin wound the reins around the brake lever and lounged into a more comfortable posture along the seat of the Beamish wagon. And caressed the stock and barrel of his Winchester rifle with movements of his filthy hands that came close to being sensual. Then he shook his head slowly from side to side: a moment later the motion of shaking taken up by his entire body which was clad in ill made, torn and stained, never mended nor laundered clothing. The neglected condition of his attire serving to emphasise the newness of the rifle he held.

Suddenly, with an abruptness that drew gasps from a number of people in the captive crowd, he curtailed the almost silent laughter. And raised a hand to knock on to the back of his head the battered and sweat stained plainsman hat that had previously shaded his ugly, time lined and element burnished features. And then he caused several of the more nervous people in the crowd to flinch, or cling to a loved one, as he raked his glaring eyes over them.

'You hear what that land grabbin' sonofabitch is callin, us?' he demanded. 'Me and my boys is creeps and you folks is critters!'

'Sleppin, you sonofabitch, that ain't what I said at all!' Jackson shrieked. 'And it ain't me that's the land grabber! I didn't roust decent and honest folks outta their beds in the dead of night and march them under threat of gettin' their heads shot off all the way to here so – '

'Hey, deputy!' the man on the wagon beside the trail cut in shrilly, as he aimed his rifle at the sky and triggered a shot.

Aboard the wagon in the timber on the ridge to the west, Julia French gasped and shook. And snapped her head around to stare at the man who now moved to climb down off the seat. She blurted, soft against the sounds of shock from below:

'Where are you going?'

'Can't see too much from here,' the Virginian told

her, and briefly showed a grin of satisfaction. Which she failed to see, but it was not meant for her anyway. He was simply pleased with himself that he had kept the area of the wound from stiffening up during the drive along the valley. For now he could move quite freely – without putting too much strain on his upper right side – and not experience more than a mild smarting sensation. The last fresh blood to erupt had now dried on his shirt and the dressing and had sealed the hole in his flesh.

'How can I flap my mouth like you asked if you keep makin' noises with yours, uh?'

'Yeah, Avery, let the man have his say!' one of the captive farmers snarled.

Steele stopped short of the fringe of the timber, and used the barrel of the Colt Hartford to ease some brush aside and get a clear view of the scene a hundred and fifty yards down the slope. Had been at this vantage point just a few seconds when the woman came to his side.

'Sun hits those glasses of yours, we might as well yell that we're up here,' he said to her.

'I'm almost blind without them,' she protested.

'Best to be that for a short time, Julia. Than dead, which is forever.'

She quickly removed her spectacles and, without the thick lenses to magnify them, her eyes appeared remarkably small.

'Just the first couple we picked up were in line to get their heads blown off!' Sleppin was saying as Steele made a more careful survey of the scene below than he had been able to do from the wagon moving through the trees. 'You're a man that sets store by records, so let's get this one straight. Needed to get all the folks in the valley together and recallin' the way I got treated when I was last through here, knew I had to do more than just ask them polite like to attend a meetin'.'

The thick set and sandy haired Dave Gruber was among the captives, the Virginian saw. So was Willard Duff. Wayne Flannery and his son Sean. Nobody else that Steele was able to recognise. So the Jacksons – Avery, Jonas and Rose – were out of sight and probably were all in the grocery. Dora and Howard Parrish were maybe in the living quarters behind the post and telegraph office. Ths fat schoolteacher with the ink stained fingers was not in sight. Nor Nicholas and Willa French. Bart Beamish. Arlene, neither.

'Your minor problem is not in evidence, Mr Steele,' Julia pointed out, with something close to a taunt in her tone, after she had satisfied herself that her parents were not under immediate threat from the grinning gunmen.

'And like the good neighbours they are, all the folks came nice and quiet so as not to get nobody killed.'

'All you said so far is how you forced those people here, Sleppin!' Jonas Jackson shouted. 'About time you got to what you plan to do – '

'Get what's mine now my old man has passed on, horse ass!' Sleppin cut in vehemently. And powered to his feet, double handed grip on the Winchester that he swung aimlessly to left and right – causing some of the mounted horsemen as well as people in the crowd to duck and sway. 'And what's mine is every acre in this valley! One end to the other! Stole by the Jacksons from the Sleppins! And sold illegal to these folks! Which is real tough shit on these folks! On account of they're gonna have to ante up again if they wanna keep the land! Or move their asses off the places so I can sell to other folks!'

There was an outburst of shrill and angered protest from the closely grouped farmers and their families. Curtailed by the crack of another shot from the muzzle of Hal Sleppin's Winchester.

'He looks to be quite insane,' Julia French hissed in the sudden silence.

'He hasn't been sounding like the most rational of men,' Steele answered with less intensity than she had generated.

'Anything could happen!'

'Lay it on the friggin' line for them, Hal!' the harsh voiced Davidson snarled, the grin of a moment ago displaced by a scowl. 'The sun's already up high enough to give me a friggin' thirst!'

'Yeah, and that stinkin' deputy and his bunch is in the place where the only liquor's kept!' another mean faced, unshaven, filthy dirty and travel weary man agreed. 'Get the lead out, Hal! And let's get to the good times you been promisin' us – '

'Shut up! Shut your friggin' mouths the whole bunch of you! I'm top man! Top man in the whole damn friggin' valley! And I call the shots!'

While Hal Sleppin ranted, shrilly confident of his power and his ability to turn events any way he wanted, Steele allowed the brush to resume its natural shape and withdrew from the vantage point. Julia French watched him, for several moments seemed about to question him, but then decided against it – assumed the place he had left and moved aside the brush with an elegant hand. And put on her glasses.

The man standing on the foot board of the wagon beside the trail continued to harangue the people of the valley and his own men. All the time brandishing his rifle which posed no intentional threat but worried a lot of nervous people that Sleppin might fire it accidentally. While in the timber on the ridge to the west, Steele climbed carefully up on to the second Studebaker and settled himself on its seat.

At the foot of the slope one man was perhaps unhinged or more likely was experiencing the exhilarating effects of unfamiliar power – and did not have the temperament to remain stable under its influence. At the top of the same ridge, another man was able to keep firmly within bounds what might otherwise have been an overwhelming sense of disenchantment. Which found outlet only in the form of a scowl of contempt as he listened to the shrill spoken ramblings of Sleppin.

'. . . so you and the rest of them better come on outta the grocery, Jackson!' the man threatened. 'On account of if you don't, I ain't gonna take no blame for what'll happen!'

'Avery, you and the others come on out for God's sake!' a man in the captive crowd pleaded. 'Our women and children are in as much danger as – '

'Don't you think we can't see that, John!' the aged deputy countered, as the fragile looking Julia French turned to look back at where the wagon with Steele up on the seat was parked. 'But if all of us surrender to these creeps like you people did, Sleppin'll have us where he wants!'

'Right on!' Eddie Duval shrilled.

'You sonofabitch, Jackson!' Wayne Flannery snarled. 'It was you got us into this rotten mess! Now you get us out!'

'Goddamnit to hell!' Jonas Jackson shrieked. 'It's Sleppin and his bunch of no good – '

'Sun's near dried me out, Hal!' Mal Davidson cut in on the younger Jackson. 'And if I don't get me somethin' to slake my thirst pretty friggin' fast, I'm gonna – '

'No, don't!' Julia French screamed.

But the Colt Hartford cracked out a shot an instant after the hammer was thumbed back. And as he cocked the hammer again, the Virginian rasped through lips still twisted in a scowl of contempt:

'Been enough shooting off of mouths, lady.'

Fourteen

ADAM STEELE fired a second shot from where he stood on the foot board of the Studebaker. Had known, from when he rose to climb down off the wagon after they first reached this point on the ridge, that in such an attitude on this position he had a clear view of the two men he had returned to the valley to kill. Could see through the intervening partial screen of brush and tree foliage some of the other horsemen and a section of the captive group, too. But all and everybody else was of no consequence to him as he powered up from the seat, aimed the Colt Hartford from his left shoulder at the Stetson covered red head of Mal Davidson, cocked the hammer and eased back the trigger. Heard the shrill denial of the woman against the crack of the rifle. Her voice and the report sounding in isolation as a total silence was suddenly clamped down over the mass of people on the valley bottom.

Then the powerful Davidson fell sideways out of his saddle, his head abruptly much redder. And an explosion of shouted curses and shrill screams accompanied the second report from the muzzle of the Colt Hartford – this shot triggered without the waste of even part of a second. Time taken only to cock the hammer and track the rifle a few inches to the side: to bring the shock contorted rodent face of Eddie Duval into line with the sights. The bullet burrowed into his head via his right cheek and he rocked backwards, struggled to stay astride his horse by flinging himself forward; but died in the attempt and slid to the ground over the rump of his mount as the animal reared.

Julia French was screaming more words at him, her fragile features made ugly by rage. But even had he been disposed to try to understand the words she hurled at him, it was doubtful if he could have made any sense out of them against the din that rose from the valley.

Screaming and shouting and the thud of running feet as men, women and children submitted to the dictates of panic. The snorting and the beating of hooves by horses. And the opening shots in a barrage of gunfire.

For stretched seconds, Steele was not able to see the events that gave rise to the sounds of pandemonium. For he was back down on the seat of the wagon again, unsighted by the brush as he clasped the rifle between his knees, knocked off the brake lever and cracked the reins above the backs of the horses.

He did see that Julia was flailing her arms now, and glimpsed that fear had displaced fury on her pale face. But he ignored her and devoted his entire attention to driving the Studebaker from a standstill to a flat out gallop over a hundred feet of slightly uphill forest floor. Crashing it through thick brush and between trunks. Needing to fend off stinging blows from brutal branches that would have cut his face to shreds had he not held up the rifle to deflect them. Needed to crouch and grip the reins and the Colt Hartford with both hands, not trusting his right arm to have the strength to deal with either task.

Then the heavy wagon was clear of the timber, the

bolting team and racing wheels missing the now terrified woman by a dozen feet. And the Virginian, haggard face once more in its usual impassive set, was able to lodge the rifle between his thighs again and give his entire energies to holding the Studebaker on course: as his red rimmed eyes took in the scene below – revealed to him in its entirety now that he was hurling across the open slope.

Not only Davidson and Duval were sprawled on the trail. More than half the former captives were also flat to the hard packed dirt on the stretch of trail between Flannery's barn and the huddle of buildings called a town. The rest were running. Men, women and children. Singly, in pairs and in small groups. But all in one direction – eastward, away from the area where the opening gunfire had sounded. Two shots that had signalled the start of the barrage that continued now – to crack bullets toward the grocery and at the racing wagon that was on a downward course for the crowd of helpless people who had hurled themselves to the ground to get below the spray of flying lead.

From stone faced impassiveness, Adam Steele's expression altered in every line and plane to a killer's grin. Ten year old girl or fully grown adult – no matter who did the favour, it had to be repaid. And he was now out of the debt of Arlene Beamish, for he could see in vivid detail the total inertia in which Davidson and Duval lay on the trail in the morning sun – the ground stained red beneath their heads. Saw, also, as he hauled on the reins to alter the direction of the bolting team, that Nick and Willa French were safe. For the moment, anyway. Glimpsed their elderly faces set in frowns of terror at the window of the schoolhouse. Across from the grocery out of which gunshots at last started to be exploded: as Avery and Jonas Jackson took a hand in the defence of their community.

The acrid stink of exploded black powder filled the air which before had been permeated only with the fragrance of pine and the stench of terror. Gunsmoke jerked and drifted. Then the Studebaker came around in a tight turn that almost caused it to cant too far, threatening to roll it over on to its side. And the Virginian abruptly conscious of a searing pain in his upper right chest as a result of his efforts to keep control of the team, nearly did not become aware of a different kind of smell of another sort of smoke. Snatched a look over his shoulder and curled back his lips to expose his teeth in an expression that was midway between a grin and a scowl.

The contents of the Studebaker and a large section of its burlap cover were ablaze – the flames and smoke and fumes trailing out behind in the slipstream of speed. The fire fanned to greater intensity by that same speed.

Bullets cracked through the flaring and the still intact cover. Bit into the timbers. Slapped past his head. The team horses, made aware of the fire behind them at the same time as Steele – when the dangerously sharp turn wafted the stinks of the blaze across their nostrils – were driven to a greater degree of panic. And the man on the seat of the flaming wagon had to abandon consideration of all else to concentrate once more on bringing the team back under control.

Any one of a barrage of shots might have tunnelled a bullet into him. But then the smoke and the flames were between him and the men who sought to kill him.

Not so many now, because three others had been blasted from the backs of their horses to sprawl to the ground. Hit by bullets exploded from the grocery. At where the men, promised so much by the power tasting Hal Sleppin, directed their shots once again. Firing wildly from the backs of horses which were spooked like those in the wagon traces by the terrifying scents of fire.

Steele, by sheer brute strength that objectively he would have considered beyond his ability, was able to exert control over the direction the wagon took. But the horses would not respond to his demands that they should slow. They raced across the face of the hillside, parallel with the trail, going south. Heading for the side of Flannery's barn, the two horses in the traces seemingly intent upon galloping full tilt into the solid obstacle. Until the Virginian hauled on the reins to bring their heads around so that they begun to angle upwards across the slope.

Only the sounds of gunfire were able to penetrate from the outside world into the capsule of raucous bedlam that enclosed Adam Steele, the two horses and the blazing wagon. Just the closest and therefore the loudest of the gunshots? Or could it be the firing was more sporadic now?

The flames and smoke trailing Studebaker jolted and rolled and bounced straight up the valley side behind Flannery's barn. Heading for the area of timber from which it had burst into the open a few killings ago. Steele, certain that panic exhausted horses were beginning to slacken their pace on the upgrade, chanced a look over his shoulder. And on the fringes of the pall of smoke could see that the battle of the valley community was almost over – as the handful of survivors of Sleppin's bunch gave their eager to run mounts their head. Back southward. And the old and young Jackson were forced to cease firing as the people who had gone voluntarily full length to the trail now got shakily to their feet.

Then Steele felt the heat of the flames and he once again devoted his entire attention to bringing the team to a halt. And on this occasion was able to do it, the two animals jerking to a stop, snorting and tossing their heads, scraping at the ground with their hooves and quivering their sweat lathered rumps and flanks.

Hooves could be heard clattering along the trail, receding southward. As Steele half climbed and half fell off the Studebaker at which the fire crackled and roared, he looked with sweat stinging eyes after the fleeing horsemen. Saw six mounts, one of them with two men astride it. The back rider of the double had a fist extended high in the air, brandishing it. His new Winchester was gone from the fist.

Steele let his own rifle fall to the ground and stooped as if to retrieve it. But instead delved a hand through the slit in the outside of his right pants leg and drew the knife from the boot sheath. Went down on to one knee and began to saw at a trace.

The fire roared and crackled and billowed smoke with more urgency. Down at the base of the slope, voices were raised. And the Virginian thought he also heard some laughter. Then was certain he heard voices, femininely shrill, at the top of the slope.

One trace was all but sawn through and as he reached across to work on the other one, he glanced at the tree covered ridge. And saw Julia French running down toward him while Arlene Beamish followed her at an ambling walk – leading the chestnut mare.

He rasped 'Whoa,' to the horses as they made to respond violently to the snapping of the second trace. Then came upright, sliding the knife back in the sheath and picking up his rifle as parts of the same move – used the Colt Hartford as a club to knock off the wagon's brake lever.

The horses stood their ground, the almost severed trace snapped under the strain and the burning Studebaker began to roll backwards down the slope. Slowly, but gathering speed by the yard.

Steele turned and, now using the rifle as a support, lowered his rump to the ground.

'Everything my parents and I have in the world is aboard that wagon!' Julia French wailed as she came to a swaying halt beside where Steele sat.

The Studebaker hurtled straight and true from its free running starting point to the rear corner of Flannery's barn. Where it impacted with a splintering of wagon and building timbers, was partially wrecked but with enough bulk and momentum to smash through the damaged walls. Where an explosion of showering sparks found a mass of fresh fuel and the flames and smoke leapt and billowed high enough to blot out the sun and cast a dark shadow across the surrounding area of the valley.

'I have a different sense of values to most people, Julia,' the Virginian finally replied wearily as the initial impetus of the barn fire diminished. 'Chose the lives of the horses ahead of the wagon.'

He had been aware of Arlene Beamish approaching where he sat and the woman stood as the barn started to burn. Also of a large group of the local citizenary trekking up the hill.

'You did what I asked, mister,' the small girl said

evenly. 'Killed the men who murdered our parents. I shouldn't have your horse as well.'

She drew the chestnut mare closer, so that she could release the reins and they hung down to drape the Virginian's aching and blood drenched upper right chest.

'A deal's a deal, kid,' he told her, still gazing at the burning barn, and wondering idly if the heat inside was any hotter than that in the area of his wound.

'But it wasn't no part of the deal for me to light the fire in the back of the wagon, mister,' the girl argued.

'I tried to warn you, Mr Steele,' the woman explained. 'I guess you didn't hear what I was – '

'But all that talk back and forth was riling me some, I can tell you,' Arlene cut in, impatient to have her say. 'I figured somebody had to do something to start things moving. But I'm just a kid. All through the night when I saw how those men were rounding up the folks I tried to think of something that would help. But I was scared to start anything on my own. In case it got anyone killed.'

'And what you done, kid, it could've!' the bearded Avery Jackson accused bitterly. 'Decent folks, I mean. But you was lucky. Just a couple of flesh wounds won't nobody die of. The five dead Sleppin men is something nobody hereabout is likely to give a hoot about.'

He shot expectant glances to either side of him. But for long moments drew no response from his fellow valley citizens, until Wayne Flannery growled:

'Figured you'd be fresh out of talk, Jackson. After all that you done with that guy reckons you cheated him and us.'

'Now you listen here – ' the elderly deputy started.

But curtailed the protest as Steele rose cautiously to his feet.

From the crowd of people, many of whom looked as haggard as Steele in the sunlight that now punched through the diminishing smoke of the barn fire, Nicholas French allowed:

'Don't hold the wreckin' of my wagon against anyone, son. Situation was starting to get real ugly and somebody had to do somethin'.'

There was a murmuring of agreement with this.

'What I said,' the freckle faced ten year old girl reminded. 'And kept on recalling what father said a lot. That if you wanted some folks to get on and move, sometimes the only way to do it was light a fire under them.'

She began a wan smile, but then her expression changed totally and she wailed as she turned toward Julia: 'There just isn't anything funny about any of this, is there?'

She buried her suddenly tearful face against the hip of the woman who took the girl's head in her two hands and held it there.

Wayne Flannery shifted his severe gaze from the black bearded deputy to the bone tired Virginian. And said in a grim tone: 'You was around when someone like you was needed, mister. More time passes, more me and some others are likely to start thinkin' about you outside of that. About Moses Jackson and the Widow Perry and them others that got killed a while back. And about how the cards could've fell different and we could have worse than two people with scratches. And me, personal, might get to thinkin' that you pointed that wagon at my barn deliberately. Even though I had nothin' to do with lockin' you up in there.'

'Now who's doin' all the damn jawin', Wayne Flannery?' Emma Gruber called sourly from the crowd.

Steele nodded and moved to the left side of the horse. And needed once more to consciously summon all his energy to complete a simple chore – that of swinging up astride the mare without displaying what it cost him. But it was not until he was in the saddle that he realised the stirrups were still set for a ten year old girl.

Julia saw this, eased away from Arlene and moved to adjust the stirrups for the sick with weariness man. And as the crowd began to disperse, she whispered to him:

'Want to thank you, Mr Steele.'

'Didn't think I did anything for you, Julia,' he said. And slid the Colt Hartford in the boot then unhooked a canteen and drank from the cool, sweet water in it.

'Refilled it from the stream last night, mister,' Arlene Beamish reported as she moved to join her acne faced brother who was going down the hill with the parents of the woman. 'No charge. And that horse was too big for me, anyway.'

Steele acknowledged this with a nod as he recorked the canteen and hung it back from the horn.

'Mr and Mrs French!' the small girl called eagerly. 'You and the other folks have to be told it was all lies about me being kidnapped by – '

'I told everybody already, Arlene,' her brother announced proudly.

'Sh . . . oooot!' Arlene countered bitterly.

'Last night, when we were resting in the ravine,' Julia went on after an impatient wait. 'Another man might have tried to sweet talk me into . . . into . . . well, you know. But you chose to rile me into realising you and I are not . . . not compatible. You know what I mean, Mr Steele?'

'Reckon so,' he answered, and heeled the mare forward, heading south.

'Perhaps under different circumstances, it would have been different!' she called after him.

'I'll keep that in mind, Julia,' he answered without looking back through the morning cleared of visible traces but still tainted with the acrid odour of smoke. 'Maybe when I get to feeling a new man, I'll . . .

. . . SEE YOU AROUND.'*

*Adam Steele, restored to full health, will certainly be around in the next book of the series.